Hezekiah Butterworth

Poems for Christmas, Easter, and New Year's

Hezekiah Butterworth

Poems for Christmas, Easter, and New Year's

ISBN/EAN: 9783743420823

Manufactured in Europe, USA, Canada, Australia, Japa

Cover: Foto ©Andreas Hilbeck / pixelio.de

Manufactured and distributed by brebook publishing software (www.brebook.com)

Hezekiah Butterworth

Poems for Christmas, Easter, and New Year's

POEMS

FOR

CHRISTMAS, EASTER, AND NEW YEAR'S.

POEMS

FOR

CHRISTMAS, EASTER, AND NEW YEAR'S.

BY

HEZEKIAH BUTTERWORTH.

FULLY ILLUSTRATED.

BOSTON:
ESTES AND LAURIAT, PUBLISHERS,
299-305 WASHINGTON STREET.
1885.

Cambridge:

PRINTED BY JOHN WILSON AND SON,

UNIVERSITY PRESS.

CONTENTS.

THE TAPER.

[INTRODUCTION.]

I.

I stood in the old Cathedral
Amid the gloaming cold;
Before me was the chancel
And unlit lamps of gold.

II.

From the mullioned window's chalice
Was spilled the wine of light,
And across the winter valleys
Was drawn the wing of night.

III.

The frescos of the angels
Above me were unseen,
And viewless were the statues
Each pillared arch between.

IV.

The chancel door swung open;
There came a feeble light,
Whose halos like a mantle
Fell over the acolyte.

V.

And one by one he kindled
The silver lamps and gold,
And the old Cathedral's glories
Before my eyes unrolled.

VI.

The jet of light was feeble;
The lamps were stars of flame;
And I could read behind them
Immanuel's wondrous name.

VII.

The taper — light's evangel —
Touched all the chandeliers;
As if by Heaven transfigured,
Appeared the Saints and seers.

VIII.

Along the sculptured arches
Appeared the statues dim;
And pealed the stormy organ
The peaceful advent hymn.

IX.

And as the form retreating
Passed slowly from my sight,
Eclipsed in lights it kindled
Was lost the taper's light.

X.

One taper lights a thousand,
  Yet shines as it has shone,
And the humblest light may kindle
  A brighter than its own.

XI.

And if within these pages,
  One touch of sympathy
May to a heart more helpful
  An inspiration be,

XII.

Not vainly moves the taper
  O'er life's cathedral floor,
Though it may pass unheeded
  Without the chancel door.

28 WORCESTER STREET, BOSTON.

THE FOUNTAIN OF YOUTH: PASCHA FLORIDA.

A DREAM OF PONCÉ DE LEON.

I.

A STORY of Poncé de Leon,
  A voyager, withered and old,
Who came to the sunny Antilles,
  In quest of a country of gold.
He was wafted past islands of spices,
  As bright as the Emerald seas,
Where all the forests seem singing,
  So thick were the birds on the trees:
The sea was as clear as the azure,
  And so deep and so pure was the sky
That the jasper-walled city seemed shining
  Just out of the reach of the eye.

By day his light canvas he shifted,
  And rounded strange harbors and bars;
By night, on the full tides he drifted,
  'Neath the low-hanging lamps of the stars.

Near the glimmering gates of the sunset,
  In the twilight empurpled and dim,
The sailors uplifted their voices,
  And sang to the Virgin a hymn.
"Thank the Lord!" said De Leon, the sailor,
  At the close of the rounded refrain;
"Thank the Lord, the Almighty, who blesses
  The ocean-swept banner of Spain!
The shadowy world is behind us,
  The shining Cipango, before:
Each morning the sun rises brighter
  On ocean, and island, and shore.

And still shall our spirits grow lighter,
  As prospects more glowing unfold;
Then on, merry men! to Cipango,
  To the west, and the regions of gold!"

II.

There came to De Leon, the sailor,
  Some Indian sages, who told
Of a region so bright that the waters
  Were sprinkled with islands of gold.

And they added: " The leafy Bimini.
  A fair land of grottos and bowers.
Is there: and a wonderful fountain
  Upsprings from its gardens of flowers.
That fountain gives life to the dying.
  And youth to the aged restores;
They flourish in beauty eternal.
  Who set but their foot on its shores!"
Then answered De Leon, the sailor:
  " I am withered, and wrinkled. and old:
I would rather discover that fountain.
  Than a country of diamonds and gold."

III.

Away sailed De Leon, the sailor,
  Away with a wonderful glee,
Till the birds were more rare in the azure,
  The dolphins more rare in the sea;
Away from the shady Bahamas,
  Over waters no sailor had seen,
Till again on his wondering vision,
  Rose clustering islands of green.
Still onward he sped till the breezes
  Were laden with odors, and lo!
A country embedded with flowers.
  A country with rivers aglow!
More bright than the sunny Antilles.
  More fair than the shady Azores.
" Thank the Lord!" said De Leon, the sailor.
  As feasted his eye on the shores.
" We have come to a region, my brothers.
  More lovely than earth, of a truth:
And here is the life-giving fountain,—
  The beautiful fountain of youth."

IV.

Then landed De Leon, the sailor,
   Unfurled his old banner, and sung:
But he felt very wrinkled and withered.
   All around was so fresh and so young.

The palms, ever-verdant, were blooming,
   Their blossoms e'en margined the seas;
O'er the streams of the forests, bright flowers
   Hung deep from the branches of trees.
" 'T is Easter," exclaimed the old sailor;
   His heart was with rapture aflame;
And he said: " Be the name of this region
   As Florida given to fame.
'T is a fair, a delectable country,
   More lovely than earth, of a truth;
I soon shall partake of the fountain, —
   The beautiful fountain of youth!"

v.

But wandered De Leon, the sailor,
   In search of that fountain in vain;
No waters were there to restore him
   To freshness and beauty again.
And his anchor he lifted, and murmured,
   As the tears gathered fast in his eye,
" I must leave this fair land of the flowers,
   Go back o'er the ocean, and die."
Then back by the dreary Tortugas,
   And back by the shady Azores,
He was borne on the storm-smitten waters
   To the calm of his own native shores.
And that he grew older and older,
   His footsteps enfeebled gave proof:
Still he thirsted in dreams for the fountain, —
   The beautiful fountain of youth.

VI.

One day the old sailor lay dying
   On the shores of a tropical isle,
And his heart was enkindled with rapture,
   And his face lighted up with a smile.

He thought of the sunny Antilles,
  He thought of the shady Azores,
He thought of the dreamy Bahamas,
  He thought of fair Florida's shores.
And, when in his mind he passed over
  His wonderful travels of old,
He thought of the heavenly country,
  Of the city of jasper and gold.
" Thank the Lord ! " said De Leon, the sailor,
  " Thank the Lord for the light of the truth,
I now am approaching the fountain, —
  The beautiful fountain of youth."

VII.

The cabin was silent : at twilight
  They heard the birds singing a psalm,
And the wind of the ocean low sighing
  Through groves of the orange and palm.
The sailor still lay on his pallet,
  'Neath the low-hanging vines of the roof;
His soul had gone forth to discover
  The beautiful fountain of youth.

MAGDALENA.

[EASTER.]

I.

MAGDALENA! Magdalena!
Hasten, feet of Magdalena!
Hasten, for the sun is rising
  O'er the Eastern hills of bloom!
In thine eyes the teardrops tender,
In thy face the morning splendor;
Hasten, feet of Magdalena,
  Hasten, hasten to the tomb!

II.

Magdalena! Magdalena!
  Once thy soul was demon-haunted,
Like the hart pursued it panted
  For the rest earth could not lend;
Then He came to thee, the Healer,
Came the Paraclete Revealer,
At His feet thou fellest, pleading,
  In His bosom found a friend.

III.

Magdalena! Magdalena!
  Thou His sandalled feet hast followed,
Thou beside His cross hast trembled,
  Hasten with the rich perfume!

Hasten with thy box of spices,
Dreaming of the Paradises,
Gardens of the halls immortal,
   Blooming far beyond the tomb!

IV.
Magdalena! Magdalena!—
   Angels speak to Magdalena.—

" Lo, the sealèd tomb is riven,
  Lo, the stone away is rolled!"
Once thy soul was demon-driven,
Now the shining ones of heaven,
By the empty tomb of Jesus,
  Thou art worthy to behold.

v.

Magdalena! Magdalena!
  Favored thou above all women,
Hasten to the sad eleven,
  To the sorrowing ones, and say,—
" He is risen! at the portal
Of His tomb are forms immortal;
Lo, mine eyes have seen the vision,
  In the place where Jesus lay!"

VI.

Magdalena! Magdalena!
  Though thy feet may flee from Judah,
Though thou diest in the caverns
  'Neath the purple skies of Gaul,
Yet thy message from the angel
Shall become the world's evangel,
And all wondering nations hear it,
  And thy mission blessèd call.

IN CHALEUR BAY.

THE birds no more in door-yard trees are singing,
  The purple swallows all have left the eaves,
And, thwart the sky, the broken clouds are winging,
  Shading the landslopes bright with harvest sheaves.
Old Hannah waits her sailor-boy's returning.
  His fair young brow to-day she hopes to bless;
But sees the red sun on the hill-tops burning,
  The flying cloud, the wild, cold gloominess
            Of Chaleur Bay.

The silver crown has touched her forehead lightly
  Since last his hand was laid upon her hair:
The golden crown will touch her brow more brightly
  Ere he again shall print his kisses there.
The night comes on, the village sinks in slumber,
  The rounded moon illumes the water's rim;
Each evening hour she hears the old clock number,
  But brings the evening no return of him
            To Chaleur Bay.

She heard low murmurs in the sandy reaches,
  And knew the sea no longer was at rest.
The black clouds scudded o'er the level beaches,
  And barred the moonlight on the ocean's breast.
The night wore on, and grew the shadows longer;
  Far in the distance of the silvered seas
Tides lapped the rocks, and blew the night-wind stronger,
  Bending the pines and stripping bare the trees
         Round Chaleur Bay.

Then Alice came: on Hannah's breast reclining,
  She heard the leaves swift whistling in the breeze,
And, through the lattice, saw the moon declining
  In the deep shadows of the rainy seas.
The fire burned warm; upon the hearth was sleeping
  The faithful dog that used his steps to follow.
" 'T is almost midnight," whispered Alice, weeping,
  While blew the winds more drearily and hollow
         O'er Chaleur Bay.

Then Hannah told old tales of France: strange stories
  Of Cinq-Mars' fall; of Richelieu's grand dreams:
Of fair chateaus: of art's triumphal glories
  In old Versailles; of brave Jacques Cartier's schemes;
Of lost Port Royal and its winter palace;
  How her dead husband's family had shone
In arts provincial. Glowed the cheek of Alice,
  And half her thoughts went wandering to the Rhone
         From Chaleur Bay.

No organ stands beneath a bust of Pallas,
  No painted Marius to the ruin clings,
No Ganymede, borne up from airy Hellas,
  Looks through the darkness 'neath the eagles' wings.

But the sweet pictures from the shadowed ceiling
   Reflect the firelight near old Hannah's chair, —
One a fair girl with features full of feeling,
   And one a boy, a fisher, young and fair,
       Of Chaleur Bay.

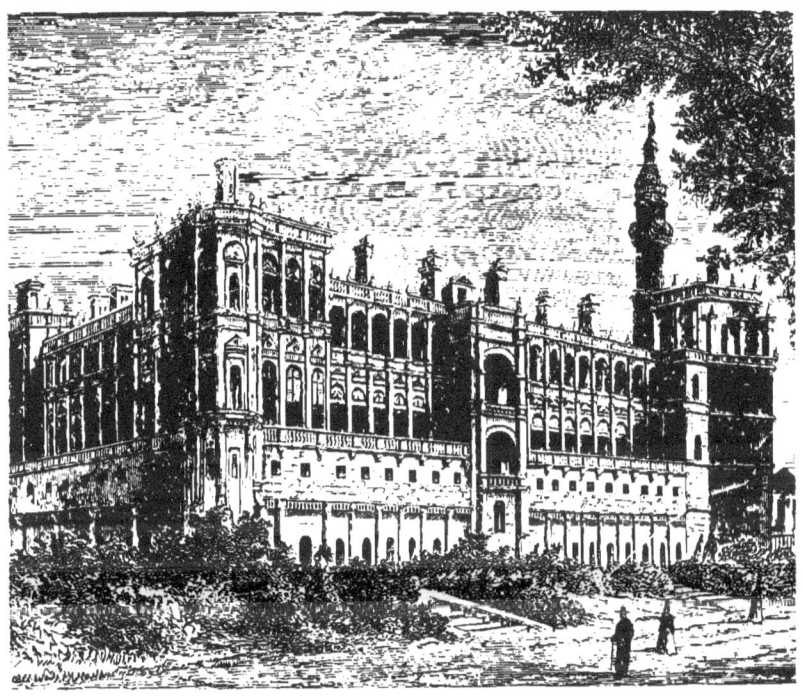

That boy returns with humble presents laden,
   And when the bells ring out on Christmas morn,
To the old church he hopes to lead the maiden,
   And with one jewel her white hand adorn.
Now Hannah drops her cheek — the maiden presses, —
   "He will return when come the morning hours,
And he will greet thee with his fond caresses.
   And thou shalt meet him diademed with flowers."
       Sweet Chaleur Bay!

Gray was the morning, but a light more tender
  Parted at last the storm-clouds' lingering glooms.
The sun looked forth in mellowness and splendor,
  Drying the leaves amid the gentian blooms,
And wrecks came drifting to the sandy reaches,
  As inward rolled the tide with sullen roar;
The fishers wandered o'er the sea-washed beaches
  And gathered fragments as they reached the shore
        Of Chaleur Bay.

Then Alice, with the village maidens roaming
  Upon the beaches where the breakers swirl,
Espied a fragment mid the waters foaming,
  And found a casket overlaid with pearl.
It was a treasure. "Happy he who claimed it,"
  A maiden said; "'t is worthy of a bride."
Another maid "the ocean's dowry" named it,
  But gentle Alice, weeping, turned aside —
        Sad Chaleur Bay! —

And went to Hannah with the new-found treasure,
  And stood again beside the old armchair;
The maids stood round her radiant with pleasure,
  And playful wove the gentians in her hair.
Then Hannah said, her feelings ill dissembling,
  "Some sailor lad this treasure once possessed;
And now, perhaps," she added, pale and trembling,
  "His form lies sleeping 'neath the ocean's breast
        In Chaleur Bay."

Now on her knee the opened box she places,
  Her trembling hand falls helpless to her breast,
Into her face look up two pictured faces, —
  The faces that her sailor-boy loved best.

One picture bears the written words, " My Mother,"
  Old Hannah drops her wrinkled cheek in pain :
" Alice " — sweet name — is writ beneath the other, —
  Old Hannah's tears fall over it like rain.
              Dark Chaleur Bay !

The spring will come, the purple swallow bringing,
  Fair Easters bloom where Christmas snowflakes fell,
But nevermore the time of flowers and singing
  Will hope revive in her poor heart to dwell.
Life ne'er had brought to her so dark a chalice,
  But from her lips escaped no bitter groan ;
They mid the gentians made the grave of Alice,
  And Hannah lives in her old cot alone
              On Chaleur Bay.

ADVENT.

I.

THE world is very blest.
All bright in east and west,
  Christ's kingdom shines.
His name new nations take,
His song new lands awake;
For him the gods forsake
  Their golden shrines.

II.

His ransomed armies march
'Neath heaven's melodious arch;
  We follow on.
Lead on, O Cross of Light.
From conquering height to height,
And add new triumphs bright
  To triumphs won.

III.

The bright years onward sweep,
That met on Patmos' steep
  The prophet's view.
A fuller song of praise
Each year the earth shall raise
Till Paradisic days
  Begin anew.

IV.

Then ever hail the birth
That made the gladdened earth
   Immanuel's.
In wider circles sweet,
Each year around his feet,
Let choral hosts repeat,
   "God with us dwells!"

THE OLD MAN'S CHRISTMAS.

A BALLAD.

"Though I'm lonely, my young daughter
Now lives happy, far away." — *Old Ballad.*

I.

HE sat by his cottage fire and dreamed, —
The poor man, feeble and old;
The silver locks o'er his shoulders streamed;
Fourscore years ago they were gold,
Poor man,
Fourscore years ago they were gold.

II.

He thought of his wife in the churchyard lone,
He thought of his children three:
They too were gone with the years, save one,
And far away was she,
Poor man,
And far away was she.

III.

He heard the winds of the sandy dunes
Pipe wearily by the sea.
He heard the moans and the hollow tones
Of the waves of the Zuyder Zee,
Poor man,
And all alone was he.

IV.

But he smiled, and the fire on his calm face shone;
  And he said, " 'T is Christmas Day,
And though I am poor, forgotten, and lone,
  She is happy far away,
      Sweet girl,
  She is happy, far away.

V.

" The household lights burn bright and clear
  In the city over the sea,
But the night is dark by Haarlem Meer,
  And cold by the Zuyder Zee,
      Ah me,
  'T is cold by the Zuyder Zee.

VI.

" She sits, perchance, 'neath the astral's light,
  And hears the city's bells,
Or sings in the crowded church to-night,
  Where the organ's anthem swells,
      Sweet girl,
  Where the organ's anthem swells.

VII.

" Her mother's eyes, her hair of gold,
  I seem again to see;
Does she think to-night of her father old,
  Does she ever think of me,
      Dear girl,
  Does she ever think of me ?"

I.

The northern winds pipe round the morgue
In the city's suburbs lone,
And mid the gloom in a desolate room
Lies a fair dead form alone,
　　　　Poor girl,
In the silent morgue, alone.

II.

"She was a shop-girl," said the guard,
As he closed the iron door.
"She lived alone, and her lot was hard,
And we know nothing more,
　　　　Poor girl:
Such things have been before.

III.

"They found her sick in the windy street,
They heard her sob and moan:
But she only said, as her spirit fled,
'My father is all alone,
　　　　Poor man,
My father is all alone!'

IV.

"God pity the old man, all alone;
God pity the fair young form,
That will add a grave to the graves unknown,
To-day in the pitiless storm,
　　　　Poor girl,
To-day in the pitiless storm."

May the Advent bells that ring over the snows
　Bring comfort to such as these.
Alas for the sorrow no man knows,
　For the sadness no man sees!
　　　　Alas and alas,
　For the sadness no man sees!

The household fires burn bright and clear
　In life's cities over the sea ;
But the nights are dark by Haarlem Meer,
　And cold by the Zuyder Zee,
　　　　Ah me!
Wherever the helpless be.

THE GOLDEN STAR.

[CHRISTMAS.]

I.

THEY brought to the cradle their gifts of gold,
  The gums of Araby sweet,
And scattered them where the stars had rolled
  Round the Babe of Bethlehem's feet.

II.

They had marched by night 'neath the diademed sky
  From the mountain-peaks afar.
But why did the heathen first descry
  The light of the Golden Star?

III.

O mystery of the nights of bliss,
  Fair nights of the Golden Star!—
The Lord is love, and the world is his,
  And all nations his children are.

IV.

Or whether he holds or breaks his seals,
  He is near to all watchful eyes.
And to those on the mountain-tops reveals
  The messages of the skies.

FAIR MORN OF THE AGES.[1]

[EASTER.]

I.

FAIR morn of the ages, the sealed tomb is broken;
  Proclaim it, melodious chimes;
The wonderful word has the Magdalene spoken,
  The hope of all people and times!

II.

The chorus cherubic bends rapturously o'er Him,
  The gates are uplifted above:
The nations are hasting to hail and adore Him,
  And share the long reign of His love.

[1] By permission of John Church & Co.

III.

Now to their bright altars are gladdened hands bringing
　Fair buds from the life-giving seed;
And palm-lands to pine-lands are joyously singing,
　"The Saviour is risen indeed!"

IV.

Sing, children of light, sing that wonderful hour;
　And perish, earth's oracles vain;
No prophet like Jesus o'er death had the power
　To rise in life's beauty again.

V.

Burst, burst into bloom then, ye gardens of roses;
　Sing, voices of spring, in the light;
Peace falls from the palms of the Christ, and discloses
　His tomb, immortality's light!

THE MARCH OF THE MAGI.

WE wait upon the mountains.
Above us shine the golden lamps of God.
      'T is silent night,
And we, the Magi, worshippers of fire,
Renew the altars that have burned undimmed
Upon these mountain tops a thousand years.
Feed ye the flames, and sing —

> "*I shall see Him, but not near,*
>   *Shall behold Him, but not nigh.*
> *A Star shall rise from Jacob*
>   *And fill the midnight sky!*
> *And here upon the mountains*
>   *Our altar-fires shall burn,*
> *Until that Star of Jacob*
>   *Afar our steps shall turn!*"

      Hail, splendid orbs!
God scatters ye like seeds in space, to bloom
In the wide gardens of heaven's flaming halls.
The firmament grows bright, a crystal floor,
An ocean quivering with celestial fire.

      Our fathers worshipped God
Amid the palaces of the Persepolis.
The city was the glory of the sun,
The crown of all the cities of the world.

'T is vanished now; her palaces
are dust;
The slimy lizards fill her broken
pavements;
Vanished are her kings.

Hail, splendid orbs!
Our father's eyes beheld thee, —
all the great
Of earth, the earliest born of
men. All hail!
Our father Abraham watched thee
night by night,
In Mesopotamian tents. Jacob
beheld
Thy silent marches under Mamre's
oak:
Joseph, at On. Zoroaster, priest
of God.
Thy mysteries read: and he did
prophesy
Another star should rise, and fill
the sky
With brightness, and the earth
forevermore
With wonder. Feed ye the flames,
and sing: —

" I shall see Him, but not near,
Shall behold Him, but not nigh.
A Star shall rise from Jacob,
And fill the midnight sky!
And here upon the mountains
Our altar-fires shall burn,
Until the Star of Jacob
Afar our steps shall turn!"

A thousand years
Upon the mountain-tops the holy seers
Have watched the rising stars, O weary nights.
It does not come; it does not yet appear.
The wondrous nights go on, and on, and on.
We feed the fires and watch, and it will come,
For God is God.

The altars blaze
And lift their splendors in night's shadowy halls.
We keep the watch our fathers left to us,
And sing the song our poet-prophet sang,
And that the priests of Baal have sung with hope,
Through all the vanished nights of vanished years.

Behold yon light!
It rises: wondrous sight, — a star. a cross,
A coronet of fire!

———

Let the altars die.
Our watch is ended. Lo, it westward moves.
Let us descend the mountain-stairs, and hence
The glorious portent follow. Farewell,
Ye flaming heights, we go to lands unknown,
Towards the Jordan. Yet once more, O priests,
The song of Balaam sing:—

> "*I shall see Him. but not near,*
>   *Shall behold Him, but not nigh.*
> *A Star shall rise from Jacob,*
>   *And fill the midnight sky!*
> *And here upon the mountains*
>   *Our altar-fires shall burn,*
> *Until the Star of Jacob*
>   *Afar our steps shall turn!*"

THE TEARS OF THE POOR.

I.

THE city was dark, and the night wind blew dreary.
  The lamps dimly burned in the mist and the sleet:
I longed for my home, with my day's work aweary.
  And homeward was turning, with hurrying feet.
I was thinking of life and its fortunes that vary.
  Its paths that are narrow, its ways that are broad:
When a hand touched my own, and a voice faltered. "Mary
  In the name of sweet Mary, the mother of God.
    Pity, oh, pity the tears of the poor!"

II.

Impatient I turned, but a moment I tarried
  (The creed was not mine the petition expressed). —
I saw the white face of a mother who carried
  A half-covered babe on her half-covered breast:
Then I passed on my way, but a burden fell on me.
  And heavier grew as the lone street I trod.
And I still seemed to feel that white hand laid upon me.
  "In the name of sweet Mary, the mother of God.
    Pity, oh, pity the tears of the poor!"

III.

More dark grew the night and the north wind more dreary.
  As backward I turned, — in the lamplight she stood.
And swayed in the mist. with her burden aweary.
  And helplessly asked for a morsel of food.

In Christ's name I gave her the help sorely needed,
 When a word from her quivering lips made me start:
"And was it the name of the Lord that you heeded,
 Or the name of the Mother that softened the heart,
 And led you to pity the tears of the poor?"

IV.

Then homeward I hurried, light-hearted and cheery,
 Though keen blew the winds through the trees thickly iced,
For happiness comes to the way-worn and weary,
 Who stop like the feet of Samaria's Christ.
And I said, "Though the creed and the ritual vary,
 O'er man's narrow bounds are the wants that are broad;
And sorrow will cry to some deified Mary,
 If heed not compassion the name of the Lord,
 Nor pauses to pity the tears of the poor."

THE DOOR OF DEATH IS THE DOOR TO LIFE.[1]

I.

As the timid feet of the Magdalene came
  To the tomb of the Lord in the silence of night,
The morning enkindled its rosy flame,
  And crystal stars paled in the orient light.
The darkness fled like the darkness of sin,
  The silent light rose like the gospel day ;
Lo! the tomb was open! And nought therein
  Of the Lord of Life but the cerements lay!

II.

While yet was silent and lone the night,
  While yet was the dome of heaven starred,
From the throne on high came the angel of light,
  And the tomb of the Lord of Life unbarred.
Then the women came to the garden in awe,
  As the flush of morn on the far hills shone ;
Seeking the dead mid the living, and saw
  But the empty rock and the sealèd stone.

III.

Then Mary wept at death's silent door,
  And waged with the doubt of her heart a strife :
And knew not the promise, that " evermore
  The door of death is the door to life !' "

1 By permission of John Church & Co.

Oh, ye who weep at death's silent door,
   And wage with the doubts of your hearts a strife,
The Lord is risen! and evermore
   The door of death is the door to life!

IV.

O Mary of Magdala! thou shalt hear
   Thy sweet name breathed by the Lord again,
And worship his feet as they draw anear,
   To lift from thy bosom its load of pain.
Our friends may vanish, the tomb may close,
   And bitterness wage in our hearts its strife;
They have risen in Jesus, and live with those
   Who have passed through the portals of death to life!

V.

Then weep no more at death's silent door,
   Nor wage with the doubt of thy heart a strife;
Remember the promise, that " evermore
   The door of death is the door to life!"
Oh, ye who weep at death's silent door,
   And wage with the doubts of your hearts a strife,
The Lord is risen! and evermore
   The door of death is the door to life!

GUILLAUME.

CHRISTMAS AT DOVER.

OH, light was the heart of Duke William,
    The minstrels all playing with glee,
His fleet dancing bright on the Channel,
    And Normandy sunk in the sea;
Above him, the sky of September,
    Below him the waters at rest,
And snowy sails breaking around him
    The light of the opaline west:
The thousand ships dropping their pennons.
    The gonfalons waving in view,
His ensign, the Normandy Lions,
    Rolled out from the mast in the blue.
"Do you see," said the Duke to the nobles,
    "The green island rising afar?
Its forests are broader and fairer
    Than those of old Normandy are.
A thousand prows cleaving the ocean
    Ten thousand men bear to the foe,
And soon in yon forests the hunters
    The Normandy bugle shall blow."

Oh, hard was the battle that followed!
    The Normans. as reddened the air
The moon of the golden September.
    Bowed down on the meadows in prayer:

They sang the great war-song of Roland
　When morning uplifted its light,
And the three Norman Lions victorious
　Waved over the carnage at night.
The standards of England were taken
　Mid plumed arrows falling like rain,
And King Harold, discrowned and forsaken,
　Was found in heaps of the slain.
Then over the Thames and the Severn,
　And over the Humber and Dee,
From the Cape of the North to the Channel
　Waved the Lions of Normandy three.

Years passed: at the Castle of Dover
　King William his Christmas-tide kept.
And when the long banquet was over,
　To the turret in loneliness crept.
The Cinque Ports were calm, and the monarch
　Gazed over the sea as of old,
And he sighed as the past rose before him
　In memories clouded and cold.

I remember Falaise and the songs that we sung
When eventide gathered the old and the young,
And over the vineyards the golden moon hung,
   In the years that are fled.

My fleet on the waters again I behold,
The gonfalons waving, the pennons of gold,
The three bannered Lions of Normandy old,
   As in years that are fled.

I pointed to England, and proudly behind
The wings of a thousand ships rose on the wind.
And the sun, sinking low. on the serried shields shined,
   In the years that are fled.

"Pevensey!" The shout from a thousand ships rung:
To Hastings we marched the green hill-sides among.
And there the great war-song of Roland we sung.
   In the years that are fled.

And calm was the evening, the moon it was round.
The dead and the dying lay thick on the ground,
As I stood by the side of young Harold discrowned.
   In the years that are fled.

My army from slumber awakened each day
The yeomen to harry. the foemen to slay.
They fought by the Humber. they fought by the Tay,
   In the years that are fled.

Fécamp glows before me. —the feasts debonair.
The troubadours' dance in the torch-lighted air.
The full wine that flowed 'neath the coronals there.
   In the years that are fled.

The scutcheon of Conqueror shines on the wall;
My triumphs are arrased in yonder bright hall;
And chronicled there, where the tapestries fall,
　　　　　Are the years that are fled.

My red wars are ending; o'er wrinkles of care
Time's coronet silver encircles my hair;
Alas and alas for the son of Robèrt,
      And the years that are fled.

Hark! . . . A young mother sings on the terrace below
To the babe on her breast an old rune of Bayeux;
My crown would I give its sweet slumbers to know,
      And to lie in its stead!

I long for my youth, for the heart of a friend,
For the peace that the palms of the Crucified send.
My conquests are dust, and darkens the end
      The years that are dead.

LIGHT-HEARTED AMID THE SNOW.

[CHRISTMAS.]

I.

THE snow-flakes fell on her golden hair
As she hied from her home away,
And bright to her as the April air
Was the shadowy Christmas day.

II.

Yes, fair as the daisied fields were the skies,
For her heart was glad and warm,
And it changed the world to a paradise,
And to blossoming air the storm.

III.

Laugh on, laugh on, O maiden fair,
  Laugh on in the storm while you may;
The snow will fall on your golden hair
  On another Christmas day.

IV.

The snow of years will fall on your hair,
  May the Christmas hope still glow,
And you will be then as free from care,
  And light-hearted amid the snow.

BLIND-MAN'S-BUFF.

[CHRISTMAS.]

KING ROBERT of the Truce of God,
Beloved alike of laic lord
   And peasant,—long his reign,—
His gold he to the needy threw:
What Christmases old Flanders knew
   And golden Acquitaine!

Peace reigned in every province fair,
And lords and knights were debonair
   In those rare days of grace.
But one lone champion won renown,
A chief who lived in Liege's town
   Beside the dimplèd Maas.

His name was Colin, and he bore
A fame no chief e'er won before,
   For blows in battle hard;
His mallet swinging in each hand,
He oft unaided slew a band,—
   They called him Jean Mallard.

He fought for loyalty and truth,
And, fighting, spent the strength of youth,
   And every foe withstood;
Till, late in life, against him rose
Count Louvain with a hundred foes,
   In Ardennes' summer wood.

The fight was hot, the fight was hard.
But 'gainst them all stood old Mallard
    And faced a hundred spears;
Till, taking him by swift surprise,
They smote his face and pierced his eyes,
    While Ardennes rung with cheers.

But, Samson-like, though blind, he dealt
Such blows as never foeman felt;
  To shun them were in vain;
This way they fled, and that they run,
But of the bravest men not one
  E'er saw the light again.

For hawk and hound in Ardennes green,
For tilting spear and gleaming scene
  Within the charmèd ring.
Young Robert led a merry court;
And far the harpers did report
  He was a merry king.

One day, upon the snow-filled dells,
Old Bruges dropped her Christmas bells,
  And gayly sung the bards.
Then called the king his sportive wights,
And bade them act, in mimic fights,
  Such deeds as old Mallard's.

They blinded one with vizor tight,
And, armed with mallet for the fight,
  He bade the others fly.
And friend and foe did he pursue,
Till king and princes from him flew,
  Each laughing merrily.

His mallet fell with rapid stroke,
And now a prince's jewels broke,
  And now a lady's pearls.
But oft the maids his stroke did miss,
And for a blow he gave a kiss,
  While laughed the captive girls.

The king repeated oft the play;
The children followed, day by day,
  In merriment as rough.
And year by year did sportive feet
On merry Christmases repeat
  The game of BLIND-MAN'S-BUFF.

When wingèd crystals fill the air,
And all the fields grow white and fair,
  And breaks the Christmas day,
The olden game of chief and lord,
Of Robert and the Truce of God,
  Well may the children play.

And like him of the kindly heart,
Let us the gold of God impart,
    To lighten want and pain.
And heart and hall will then renew
Such Christmases as Bruges knew
    And golden Acquitaine.

THE BELLS OF URI.

[NEW YEAR'S.]

[Lake Uri unites with Lake Lucerne. Each lake is surrounded with simple chapels, the bells in whose white towers were once rung during storms, in the belief that the music would dissipate them. Over both lakes rises Mt. Pilatus, dark and cloudy, on whose summit, Pontius Pilate, according to tradition, met his fate by throwing himself into one of the lakes in the region of the clouds.]

FRÄULEIN, how light the boatmen row!
    Lucerna's deeps lie still:
And Uri's bells ring sweet and low
    From distant hill to hill.
I love the calm, still lake, Fräulein,
    The songs the boatmen sing,
But drop a tear whene'er I hear
    The bells of Uri ring.

O Gretchen, Gretchen, lift thy eyes,
    The sun of night how fair!
How grandly Pilate's peaks arise
    In yon celestial air!
I love Lucerna's placid ways,
    The songs her boatmen sing;
And my heart beats light to hear at night
    The bells of Uri ring.

Fräulein, the scenes of other years
    My shadowy memory fill:
Those bells no more my father hears;
    The world for him is still.
And ever on such eves as this
    My thoughts will backward wing;
And falls the tear whene'er I hear
    The bells of Uri ring.

The moon in still Lucerna lies;
    And see, my little maid,
How fair the crystal peaks arise
    Above the Righi's shade!
The young bird seeks its nest no more
    When summer plumes its wing;
And long. as they have done before,
    Shall Uri's sweet bells ring.

Fräulein, my mother once was young,
    Like mine her heart was gay;
For her the bridal songs were sung
    On yonder hill's *châlet.*
For her, Fräulein, will come no more
    The year's returning spring;
She'll never walk with me the shore
    When Uri's sweet bells ring!

O Gretchen, Gretchen, think no more
  On that forgotten day;
When birds above the valley soar
  Their shadows flee away.
Lay gently on the old year's graves
  The Edelweiss each spring;
And smile, my dear, whene'er you hear
  The bells of Uri ring!

Fräulein, the bright days disappear;
  One day will come the spring;
Nor you nor I again will hear
  The bells of Uri ring.
Then chide me not if stormless hours
  Like these a sadness bring,
And falls the tear whene'er I hear
  The bells of Uri ring.

Ah, Gretchen, when Death's mystic night
  To thee shall angels bear,
And thou with them shalt plume thy flight
  Through life's immortal air;
When yon fair lake for thee is still,
  And other boatmen sing,
Thou 'lt shed no tear that others hear
  The bells of Uri ring!

THE EASTER BELLS IN THE MIST.

I.

The cloud from the ocean is lifting;
And my bark, as I breathlessly list,
On the refluent tides is drifting
    Towards the city of bells in the mist,
    Towards the city of bells in the mist.

II.

The ocean lies darkly behind me,
    The storms through the cordage that hissed;
And I hear, though the cloud shadows blind me,
    The music of bells in the mist,
    The music of bells in the mist.

III.

And fond hopes I cherished are bringing
    The tears that I cannot resist,

As I hear in the viewless towers ringing
  Old Trinity's bells in the mist,
  Old Trinity's bells in the mist.

IV.

Ah me, what fond hope and emotion!
  So near to the lips I have kissed!
Methinks that my life is an ocean,
  And the end but a shore in the mist,
  And the end but a shore in the mist.

V.

A haven of rest lies before me;
  And I hear through the calms, as I list,
From the city unseen rising o'er me,
  The sweet bells of Hope through the mist,
  The sweet bells of Hope through the mist.

VI.

The mist in the morning is glowing
  With a glory it cannot resist;
And calmed tides are refluent flowing
  Towards the music that falls through the mist,
  Towards the music that falls through the mist.

VII.

Parted hands, that were trustful and tender,
  Parted lips, that once fondly I kissed,
For you is the shadowless splendor,
  For me is the sail in the mist, —
  The white sail of Faith in the mist.

4

CHRISTMAS EVE IN THE CATACOMBS:

A TALE OF THE AGE OF AURELIAN.

[Christmas, according to tradition, was first celebrated in the chapels of the catacombs of Rome during the reign of Aurelian. The Roman Saturnalia was changed to the festival of Christmas after the triumph of Christianity in the West.]

Sicelides Musæ, paulo majora canamus:
Non omnes arbusta juvant humiles que myricæ:
Si canimus silvas, silvæ sint consule dignæ.
Ultima Cumæi venit jam carminis ætas:
Magnus at integro sæclorum nascitur ordo,
Jam redit et Virgo, redeunt Saturnia regna;
Jam nova progenies cœlo demittitur alto.

VIRGIL, *Pollio.*

THE CHAPEL OF THE CATACOMBS.

PART I.

THE PILGRIM OF THE NIGHT.

IN those strange days
When Christian martyrs put to flight the gods
Of Rome, the Church walked not as now with torch
Of faith inverted, and eyes bent upon
Life's outward forms.
　　　　　　　Faith scaled the walls of heaven.
The air was spanned with bows prophetic:
Men saw the Lord in earth and sea and sky;
And every cloud that crossed the sun's bright track
Appeared an angel's chariot.
　　　　　　　The festivals —
Green Christmas, lilied Easter now — were feasts
Of soul alone in the still chapels under ground.

'T was the day of the Saturnalia,
　　When War and Labor ceased:
In the porticos of the Capitol
　　Was spread the harvest feast:
Through the streets a gay procession
　　Swept like a glimmering tide:
'T was a day of Rome in her glory,
　　A day of Rome in her pride.

The clustered wine lay heavy
    In the vineyards of Tivoli.
The gardens were filled with plenty
    From Alba's hills to the sea.
And pride filled the heart of Aurelian,
    As the halls of the Capitol rung
With the lauds of the Golden Ages,
    By the bards of Saturn sung.

Night came: on the wide Campagna
    Was never a night more fair. —
The golden moon, like a goddess,
    Rode low in the golden air.
The nobles and peasants feasted,
    In the palaces, side by side;
'Twas a night of Rome in her glory,
    A night of Rome in her pride.

A white-haired man, that evening,
    Passed slowly the throngs among,
And he heard as he plodded onward,
    The lauds of Saturn sung.
Without the gates, he slowly
    Passed down the Appian Way,
To the quarries where a chapel
    'Neath the white Campagna lay.

And there, in the sea of moonlight,
    In the purple dusk and gloom,
The thin form seemed to vanish
    Like a ghost into a tomb.
He entered the Martyrs' Chapel,
    And, 'neath the torches' glare,
He bowed his head and listened
    To a sweet chant rising there.

I.

The Earth was all silent,
When, Night's crystal gates unbarred,
And bright with angels,
All the heavens were starred.

Like an orient splendor
Glowed the vision full and clear.
Then rose the Night Pilgrims,
And Bethlehem drew near.
Pilgrims,
Lone Pilgrims,
Journeying 'neath the mystic light,
Seeking,
Christ seeking,
Seeking in the Night.

II.

Pilgrims, Night Pilgrims,
On we march in spirit still,
Stars shine above us,
Songs the heavens fill.
Where is He, earth's Stranger, —
Joy and hope of all mankind?
In the heart's low manger,
Jesus seek and find.
Pilgrims,
Night Pilgrims,
Angels sing thy quest to cheer
Pilgrims,
Night Pilgrims,
Jesus still is here!

PART II.

THE CHAPEL OF THE CATACOMBS.

Night Pilgrim :
    " Peace, brothers, peace !
I come to thee once more in Jesu's name,
A pilgrim of the night. I wished to share
The Agapæ with you once more: to see
The tombs within the Martyrs' Chapel. This is
The night of our Immanuel.
     " I do remember well the day
I came to Rome. Ignatius bid me come,
And faithful Polycarp, — blessed martyrs each,
And bosom friends of the Beloved John.
     " John ! — How Polycarp loved him,
And in communion sweet with him about
The Lord, how he was drawn towards heaven !
John laid his hands on him, and bid him preach
The word in the fair city of the Ægean Sea, —
Smyrna, whose sails go out to every land.
A faithful witness to the truth was he,
A Golden Candlestick, one of the Seven.
I saw him stand *that* day amid the flames
Unbound, I saw him when he fell
Upon the fagots: his face was turned to heaven,
And filled with joy ineffable.
       " Ignatius ! —
The little child that Jesus took into
His arms and blessed ! — I well remember him,
Sent forth by John to preach in Antioch.

I heard the shout go up, the shout of hell,
In the great Coliseum, when rushed the beasts
Upon him. O Rome! Rome! his blood one day
Will be required of thee!

       " What sights I've seen!
What blessings had! John was taught of Christ,
And I by John's disciples. Christ's kingdom comes.
It shall arise from out the ruined shrines
Of Rome, for Rome shall vanish. All her gods
Shall vanish with her smoke into the air."

     The old man paused,
And gazed about him. In the garish light
Of flaming torches, here and there appeared
The emblems graven on the martyrs' tombs, —
The cross, the dove, the dove upon the cross,
And the Good Shepherd, and on every hand
The martyr's cup and palm.

Night Pilgrim:
     " Palms of victory! Shouts of glory!
Have ye not seen them waving in the streets?
Have ye not heard them filling all the air?
It's been a golden day in golden Rome.
And happy is Aurelian.

       " And now 't is night.
The full-orbed sun of night hangs in the air,
And run the jewelled cups with plenteous wine,
In the white palaces.

       " Palms of victory!
I, too, have seen and see them. *There* are palms,
Look at them on the walls: this is a bower
Of palms: it looks to me like Paradise.

     " Look, look upon the walls!
Between the sepulchres! Lo! who are these?

I hear an angel answer :

" ' These be they who have put off
Their perishable clothing, and now are crowned
With crowns immortal ; to them are given
The palms eternal ; they have overcome,
And high ascended in the light of God.' "

The old man upward looked :

"O messenger divine,
Who is this so young that crowneth them,
And gives them palms of everlasting verdure, —
Who is this so young and fair ?

Hush ! the angel :

" ' It is the Son of God whom they confessed,
Born of a Virgin, crucified for men,
Ascended into glory.'
    Look on yonder tomb,
As flares the torch before it. What do ye read ?

" ' ALEXANDER IS NOT DEAD ; HE RESTS IN CHRIST,
AND LIVES BEYOND THE STARS. HE PASSED AWAY
UNDER ANTONIUS. WHILE ON HIS KNEES
ABOUT TO SACRIFICE TO THE TRUE GOD,
THEY SUMMONED HIM TO DEATH.
                    ' ' OH, HOPELESS TIMES,
WHEN IN THE CAVERNS AND THE DENS OF EARTH
IT IS NOT SAFE TO DWELL. O HAPPY MARTYRS,
YE SHALL SHINE IN HEAVEN.'

"Yes, blessed saint,
He lives beyond the stars. There I shall live.
Thin, thin to-day has seemed the veil to me

Between my soul and the eternal city;
And as to-night I tottered on my way
And looked about, each drifting cloud appeared
An angel's car.
         " Yes, 't will be ended soon;
This mould of flesh will soon dissolve, and I
Shall join the martyrs, and receive my palm;
Christ soon is coming in the clouds for me.
In the morning when I wake I see Him near
Most wonderfully beautiful; and every night
The early vision is the last to fade.
            "It is the Saturnalia.
The city celebrates the Age of Gold.
A glory lights the temples of the Sibyl.
         " Let me prophesy:
The Age of Gold in Christ will soon begin;
Saturn will vanish and his feast will die;
And not in martyrs' chapels under ground,
But in the glorious temples of all lands,
The saints shall hold the Festival of Peace,
And hail the birth of Christ as King of kings."

     Again the old man paused.
A holy rapture seemed to fill his face, —
A light ineffable.

   " The earth shall sweep through mist and cloud,
     Through violence and wrong,
But every land shall own our Lord
     And hear the angels' song.

   " The heavenly fruit is ripe to fall,
     As spake Eseas' tongue.
Fulfil the Sibyl's dreams, and all
     Etrurian Virgil sung.

"O Night of Time, roll on, roll on,
  With Bethlehem's starry splendor,
Not ages past, but those to come,
  Shall Christ his kingdom render.

"Apollo, smitten, shall depart,
　　Minerva lone and wan;
And change the church to holy art
　　The pastoral pipes of Pan.

"And when the Rome of old renown
　　The pagans' feet have trod,
Another Rome herself shall crown,
　　With golden domes of God."

　　　　　　Still brighter grew
The Pilgrim's face: prophetic fire had touched
The altar of his heart; his lips seemed lost
For words; his thoughts were more than utterance.

"It comes! the invisible reign is appearing;
　　The armies of heaven its advent attend.
It comes! and man's spiritual vision is clearing;
　　To spirits imprisoned in flesh it descends.
　　　　It comes, lo, it comes!

"Unseen are its hosts and the war that it wages;
　　Without observation the swelling tide runs.
Then say not, Lo, here! or Lo, there! through the ages
　　It grows with all peoples, it follows all suns.
　　　　It comes, lo, it comes!

　　"The midnight hour is past.
Still flow the cups in yonder golden halls,
And we will feast from the Eternal Tables.
This is our feast of Charity.

Hark! — "
　　　　　　The old man paused.
A sound of hurrying feet was heard, and then

A ghastly face appeared, and terror seized
The silent company.

Messengers :
　　" Ye are betrayed.
The gates of Rome are closed to you forever,
The festival of peace is ended, and
Sentinels at all the city's gates
Are watching your return."

Worshippers :
　　" Then we are exiles ? "

PART III.

THE CITY OF THE STARS.

Night Pilgrim:

"Exiles?

From Rome the crown of cities? Rome, that holds
The crown of crowns of earth?
    "I see her in a vision.
All she has been for twice a thousand years,
As in a long procession, sweeps before
My eyes.
      "The Tiber flows beneath me,
And the Palatine lies dreaming in the sun.
I see Æneas bring his household gods
To Latium. I see the long slow line
Of Latin kings; the hundred Latin fathers;
Romulus; Pompilius; Tullus. I see
Grand Cincinnatus leave his plough, and win
His victory for the State, and turn again
Towards the Tiber; the Decemviri;
The Gauls, that, pouring o'er the Alps, flash down
Upon the ill-defended walls and slay
The defiant senators; the Punic wars;
The fall of Carthage; and the successive pomps
That follow her bright car of victory.
    "She now is Queen.
Corinth is hers, and Macedon and Syracuse;
Her eagles fly to devastate the world.
Now Cæsar takes the purple, and the line
Of emperors that rule the world begins.

" Your looks are sad.
Banished are we? Do ye not know, have ye not learned
There is another city, — a city of the stars?
A thousand suns blaze round its gates, and it
Shall never perish. We are pilgrims here.
    " Your looks are sad.
Listen, while I read; they are the words of Paul:

    " ' JERUSALEM WHICH IS ABOVE IS FREE,
WHICH IS THE MOTHER OF US ALL.'

    " I wait my master's summons,
As waits the Roman soldier in the light
Of the faint morning, for the trumpet's call.
    Are ye not content?

I.

    " I would not stay the years that wing,
      Howe'er my lot be cast:
Nor say, O Sun, look back and bring
      One day from out the past.
He ever will my portion be
      Whom me to Him did call:
Jerusalem above is free,
      And mother of us all.

II.

    " The doors of earth may close to me,
      Warm hearts to me grow cold,
And sympathy be strange to me
      When life is long and old.
Or well or ill, afar I see
      Fair Zion's love-lit hall:
Jerusalem above is free,
      And mother of us all.

III.

" Free are her happy gates to prayer,
  And open night and day ;
The tuneful lyres grow sweeter there
  When earth-worn pilgrims pray ;
And wakes the strain of Jubilee,
  When helpless sinners call :
Jerusalem above is free,
  And mother of us all.

IV.

" Free are the fadeless bowers of rest,
  And free their joys untold :
Free are the mansions of the blest,
  And free the streets of gold.
Though hidden long the glories be,
  Salvation is the wall :
Jerusalem above is free,
  And mother of us all.

V.

" The outcast there may find a rest,
  The lost may there be found ;
Compassion is Immanuel's breast,
  And love Immanuel's ground.
When human ears reject the plea,
  A Prince will hear the call,
For fair Jerusalem is free,
  And mother of us all.

VI.

" Above all heavens, a voice I hear
  Dispelling every doubt, —
Who comes to Me, this Pierced Hand
  Will never cast him out.

Power to become a son of God
  Awaits him at his call;
For God's own city shall be free,
  And mother of us all.

VII.

"God's City of the Stars! Thy head
  With coronals is bright,
The emerald rainbows o'er thee shed
  Their soft attempered light.
Around thee blaze a thousand suns;
  Earth's tapers, oh, how small!
And thou art to my spirit free,
  And mother of us all.

VIII.

"The ruby from the rose may fade,
  The crystal from the stream,
And jasper sunsets melt in shade
  Like jewels of a dream.
But from thy radiant walls no gem
  Shall ever fade or fall:
And thou art free, Jerusalem,
  And mother of us all.

IX.

"Soon, soon with sin the daily strife
  Will be forever o'er,
And I shall pass from life to life
  Through Mercy's open door.
My soul in fairer worlds than this
  Has built her mansion wall:
Jerusalem above is free,
  And mother of us all.

X.

" Beat on, O heart, time's latest breath
　　Has nought to cause thy fear;
Beat on, O heart, and long for death,
　　When Jesus shall appear.
When earthly fountains fail, the sea
　　Of God's great love recall:
Jerusalem above is free,
　　And mother of us all.

XI.

" O starry heights, to which my feet
　　In darkness wend their way!
O sea of peace, whose tides retreat
　　Just out of sight each day:
Through doors of Providence to me
　　I hear the Saviour call:
But thou, Jerusalem, art free,
　　And mother of us all.

XII.

" Home! home! I shall go home at last;
　　My soul the summons waits,
And day by day her journey makes
　　Around the golden gates.
The voice may call at noon; the stroke
　　At midnight hour may fall:
Jerusalem above is free,
　　And mother of us all.

XIII.

" Then close, ye gates of Rome, to me!
　　Warm hearts, to me grow cold!
Build ye the martyr's fires and free
　　The spirit from the mould.

Heir of the Cross, it matters not
  How this worn tent may fall:
The city of the stars is free,
  The mother of us all.

XIV.

" I would not stay the years that wing,
  Howe'er my lot be cast;
Nor say, O Sun, look back and bring
  One day from out the past.
He ever will my portion be,
  Whose goodness I recall;
Jerusalem above is free,
  And mother of us all."

The worshippers arose,
And Pilgrims of the Night their faces set
Towards Puteoli.
  Pilgrims,
  Night Pilgrims.
Angels sing thy quest to cheer.
  Pilgrims,
  Night Pilgrims,
Jesus still is near.'

THE TIME IS SHORT.

[NEW YEAR'S.]

I SOMETIMES feel the thread of life is slender,
And soon with me the labor will be wrought;
Then grows my heart to other hearts more tender.
        The time,
        The time is short.

A shepherd's tent of reeds and flowers decaying,
That night winds soon will crumble into nought;
So seems my life, for some rude blast delaying.
        The time,
        The time is short.

Up, up, my soul, the long-spent time redeeming;
Sow thou the seeds of better deed and thought;
Light other lamps, while yet thy light is beaming.
        The time,
        The time is short.

Think of the good thou might'st have done, when brightly
The suns to thee life's choicest seasons brought;
Hours lost to God in pleasures passing lightly.
        The time,
        The time is short.

Think of the drooping eyes thou might'st have lifted
To see the good that Heaven to thee hath taught;
The unhelped wrecks that past life's bark have drifted.
      The time,
      The time is short.

Think of the feet that fall by misdirection :
Of noblest souls to loss and ruin brought,
Because their lives are barren of affection.
      The time,
      The time is short.

The time is short. Then be thy heart a brother's
To every heart that needs thy help in aught;
Soon thou may'st need the sympathy of others.
      The time,
      The time is short.

If thou hast friends, give them thy best endeavor,
Thy warmest impulse and thy purest thought,
Keeping in mind in word and action ever
      The time,
      The time is short.

Each thought resentful from thy mind be driven,
And cherish love by sweet forgiveness bought :
Thou soon wilt need the pitying love of Heaven.
      The time,
      The time is short.

Where summer winds, aroma-laden, hover,
Companions rest, their work forever wrought;
Soon other graves the moss and fern will cover.
      The time,
      The time is short.

Up, up, my soul, the shade will soon be falling;
Some good return in later seasons wrought;
Forget thyself, at duty's angel's calling.
          The time,
          The time is short.

By all the lapses thou hast been forgiven,
By all the lessons prayer to thee hath taught,
To others teach the sympathies of Heaven.
          The time,
          The time is short.

To others teach the overcoming power
That thee at last to God's sweet peace hath brought;
Glad memories make to bless life's final hour.
          The time,
          The time is short.

BY AHAVA RIVER.

Then I proclaimed a fast there, at the river of Ahava, that we might afflict our-
selves before our God, to seek of him a right way for us, and for our little ones, and
for all our substance.

For I was ashamed to require of the king a band of soldiers and horsemen to help
us against the enemy in the way: because we had spoken unto the king, saying,
The hand of our God is upon all them for good that seek him : but his power and
his wrath is against all them that forsake him.

So we fasted and besought our God for this : and he was entreated of us. — EZRA
viii. 21-23.

THE sun had set.
The silver stars hung low, and blazed afar
Like lights around the mountains.

The Prophet rose,
He whom great Artaxerxes, king of kings,
Directed to God's temple.
His face was bright
With all the holy radiance of the soul,
And, 'neath the first month's trembling moon.
He spake of lofty faith and answered prayer.
And cheered his fellow-prophets on their way
Toward the Holy City : —

I.

"From the long captivity
Turn we, still by foes oppressed.
Through the fronded palms, I see
The veilèd splendors of the west,
And I lay me down to rest
                    By Ahava River.

II.

" But Jerusalem is far,—
City that I long to see;
And the courts of Zion are
Silent oracles to me.
Shines the evening's silver star
                    On Ahava River.

III.

"Lies before a hostile way.
Through what dangers must I go!
But my hope of help I stay
On One stronger than the foe.
Let me pray. The wind breathes low
                    On Ahava River.

IV.

"Peace is on these shadowed hills ;
Solemn peace is in the trees ;
And God's peace my spirit fills
Like the silence of the seas.
Cools the burning air the breeze
                    Of Ahava River.

V.

"On the morrow is the fast,
Solemn fast we pause to hold ;
On the Lord our burden cast

As in mighty days of old.
Mirrored is the moon of gold
      On Ahava River.

VI.

" Prayer that God will guide our feet
On the morrow shall arise.
Dreams of Hebron's clusters sweet,
Dreams of Carmel's rosy skies,
All the night shall bless our eyes
      By Ahava River.

VII.

" Dreams of fair Jerusalem,
Dreams of viol and of flute,
Bells upon the ephod's hem,
Dulcimer, and airy lute
Bless our ears, while all is mute
      By Ahava River.

VIII.

" God will keep and God will guard;
His salvation we shall see.
He shall lift his flaming sword,
And the enemy shall flee.
He will sure entreated be
      By Ahava River.

IX.

" After solemn fast and prayer,
He will answer all our need;
Stronger his protecting care
Than are Persian shield or steed.
He our exiled feet will lead
      From Ahava River.

X.

"When Jerusalem appears,
  When I see its rising wall,
Then mine eye will melt with tears,
  Then on bending knees I 'll fall,
  And the solemn fast recall
                 By Ahava River."

"Their mounds shall have our blessing of protection,
While blooming years return."

MEMORIAL DAY.

I stand upon the summer hills and listen
 To voices murmurous, low;
Beneath the slopes the havened waters glisten,
 In sunset light aglow.

So light and airy now the sunbeam tarries,
 That fancy almost sees
The zephyr's wings, half-folded, like a fairy's,
 In half-illumined trees.

A gentle spirit charms the restful hours ;
 Dews gem the pendent fern ;
Wave low the censers of eternal flowers,
 And lilied airs return.

But some that life's sweet habitudes did follow
 In golden Junes of yore,
When summer comes, and brings the purple swallow,
 Will come to us no more.

They fell beneath the tattered banners, streaming
 On battle's clouded breath,
Where heroes saw, in serried columns gleaming,
 The lurid fires of death.

They come no more when bugles deep are blowing
 On Freedom's natal days ;
They hear no more, in sweet, suave numbers flowing,
 The patriot hero's praise.

The birds sing sweetly o'er their mounds, while Sorrow
  Sees but a flower-crowned tomb;
As though death had some luminous to-morrow
  Of beauty and of bloom.

As though each life, a sacrifice to duty,
  Had vanished into light,
And risen again in other spheres of beauty,
  Beyond the shades of night.

But martyrdom has long its summer roses
  In memory's gardens fair,
And lilies white, where fragrance long reposes,
  In sun-illumined air.

Their mounds shall have our blessing of protection,
  While blooming years return,
While summer airs give flowers a resurrection,
  And gem the moss and fern.

Graves of our foes that pendent spring ferns cover,
  Brave hearts to mind that call;
Let Charity's kind memories round them hover,
  And there her roses fall.

Foes in the wrong that faced the purple terror,
  We sinned with them and fell;
In lapses long each shared the common error,
  Each faced the breath of hell.

The strife is past, its bugle-calls, its marches:
  The peans of victory cease;
Janus is closed; and o'er its silent arches
  Stands the white angel Peace.

RISEN.

(Written for Ruggles Street Church, Boston, for Sunday, March 25, 1883.)

[EASTER.]

RISEN, Christ is risen!
Hear the angel say:
Never word so glorious,
Burst upon the day!

Risen, Christ is risen!
Hear the church repeat,
As her bannered armies
Follow Jesus' feet.

CHORUS.

Risen, Christ is risen!
Hail the morning bright,
Children of the promise,
Children of the light.

Risen, Christ is risen,
Let our anthems say;
For our sake the Saviour
Rose this wondrous day.
Ours the hopes eternal
Of his empty tomb;
Ours regained the Eden
Of immortal bloom.

Tenants for a moment
Of abodes of clay,
Heirs of habitations
That shall ne'er decay,
In his resurrection
Life is but a breath,
We his feet shall follow
Through the gates of death.

Shines the wondrous morning
On the ages long!
Hail it, halls of Zion,
Glorious now with song!

Perish, mortal bodies ;
Vanish, empty breath.
Hail him,— Jesus ! Jesus!
Conqueror of death !

THE CELESTIAL PILOT.

A REMEMBRANCE OF LIVERPOOL.

I.

THE sunset light on Birkenhead
  Shines bright, above the shading seas;
And flame like oriels, gold and red,
  The western windows of the trees:
A calm is in the damask air,
And slow ships pass, with pennants fair.

II.

Alone, I walk along the quays,
  Where thousands walk each day alone,—
Sad highways by the peopled seas,
  Where travellers meet and part, unknown.
For here, beneath this gray sea-wall,
Each day an hundred anchors fall.

III.

In yonder mists, the cliffs beside,
  1 see the impatient ships afar,
That wait the Mersey's rising tide
  To lift them o'er the harbor bar,
And here, beside Victoria's Tower,
1 watch for them an idle hour.

IV.

I watch the ships that wait to go;
  I watch the ships that wait to come;
And hear the deep tides pulsing slow
  Against the sea-walls cold and dumb.
The eve is calm, the salt air cool,
And fades the light from Liverpool.

V.

The havened ships around me rise:
  I know that they were made to sail
On other seas, 'neath other skies,
  To breast the billows and the gale;
And yet they lie with folded sails,
As though there were no seas or gales.

VI.

Each ship declares the builder's plan,
  The purpose of a mind unseen.
Beyond the horizons I can scan,
  The airy mists of shade and sheen,
Their ribs of oak were made to go,
Their deftly fashioned sails to blow.

VII.

'T is so with thee, O Soul of mine:
  'T is thus 't is given thee to know,
That past earth's low horizon line
  Thou too art formed at last to go;
And there within thyself may'st find
The purpose of a higher Mind!

VIII.

They were not given thee for nought, —
  Fair Hope to leave the havened shores,
And ripe Experience like a chart,
  And Faith that highest Heaven explores:
There is another shore for thee, —
It lies beyond the silent sea.

IX.

O ports beyond the port of time,
  O fair abodes of glowing spheres,
O deeps profound, O heights sublime,
  O morns of holy atmospheres.
O orbs remote of glorious light
That here but faintly meet my sight! —

X.

Towards you my bark of life is turned,
  The morning light is on the prow.
Fair shores await thee, undiscerned,
  Ports that no dreams discover now;
And, in horizons near or far,
There shines for thee the polar star.

XI.

The tide is rising: from the quays
   The ships go out, one after one,
To breast the waves of rising seas,
   And idly drift in calms of sun.
The tide is rising: lo, afar
The white sails cross the harbor bar!

XII.

Now fast they come towards Birkenhead;
   Their free wings beat the breezes cool,
And drop their flags of commerce red
   Before the docks of Liverpool:
And lo, like God's own lamp afar,
Shines on the sea the polar star!

XIII.

The tide is rising: I shall go
   Some day beyond the refluent sea.
The mornings on the hills shall glow
   In far horizons, lost to me;
And all my powers of soul will share
A broader sea, a brighter air.

XIV.

The tide is rising: let me gain
   A freightage for the ports sublime,
That lift their splendors o'er the main
   Beyond the stormy shores of time.
The eve is calm, the sea is full,
Fast come the ships to Liverpool.

XV.

Fast come the ships: the polar star
  Has led their varying courses right,
From each pacific port afar
  To England's port of peace, to-night;
And here their sails fall peacefully.
In this calm city of the sea.

XVI.

O Polar Star, be thou my guide
  Where'er my duty bids me go;
There is no sea nor ocean tide
  Where thy fair lamp shall cease to glow;
And thou wilt rightly lead my bark
O'er seas mysterious and dark.

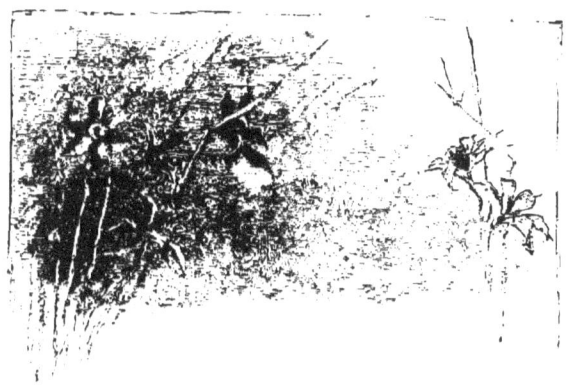

NOON OR NIGHT.

[NEW YEAR'S.]

I LOOK upon the clock.—'t is noon;
    The hour of day I know full well;
It may be noon of life with me,—
    It may be, but I cannot tell.
I cannot see the hand divine
That marks of life's short day the time.

I would not set the hand of fate
    Back on its dial: I draw near
The thousand suns whose golden gates
    Before my Saviour's throne appear.
That world I would not dare to claim
Except by faith in Jesus' name.

No night is there. The worlds below
    May wheel in darkness and eclipse:
But those celestial summits glow
    With glories whose apocalypse

The loved disciple saw awhile
On the Ægean's rocky isle.

I read the page with dazzled eye:
    What John beheld I yet shall see;
The golden gates through years may lie,
    A day may bring them close to me.
Or noon, or night, I cannot tell;
I journey on with Christ to dwell.

To overcome! to overcome!
    At noon and night shall be my prayer;
For he that overcomes at last
    Shall all the prophet's vision share.
If noon, the way is long; if night,
Fair life is near the gates of light.

THE FIRST CHRISTMAS IN NEW ENGLAND.

THAT GRAY, COLD CHRISTMAS DAY, DECEMBER 25, 1620.

I.

THEY thought they had come to their port that day,
    But not yet was their journey done;
And they drifted away from Provincetown Bay
    In the fireless light of the sun.
With rain and sleet were the tall masts iced,
    And gloomy and chill was the air;
But they looked from the crystal sails to Christ,
    And they came to a harbor fair.
        The white hills silent lay, —
    For there were no ancient bells to ring,
    No priests to chant, no choirs to sing,
    No chapel of baron, or lord or king,
        That gray, cold winter day.

II.

The snow came down on the vacant seas,
    And white on the lone rocks lay;
But rang the axe 'mong the evergreen trees,
    And followed the Sabbath day.
Then rose the sun in a crimson haze,
    And the workmen said at dawn:
" Shall our axes swing on this day of days,
    When the Lord of Life was born ?"
        The white hills silent lay, —
    For there were no ancient bells to ring,
    No priests to chant, no choirs to sing,
    No chapel of baron, or lord or king,
        That gray, cold Christmas Day.

III.

"The old towns' bells we seem to hear:
 They are ringing sweet on the Dee;
They are ringing sweet on the Harlem Meer,
 And sweet on the Zuyder Zee.
The pines are frosted with snow and sleet.
 Shall we our axes wield,
When the chimes at Lincoln are ringing sweet,
 And the bells of Austerfield?"
        The air was cold and gray, —
        And there were no ancient bells to ring,
        No priests to chant, no choirs to sing,
        No chapel of baron, or lord or king,
        That gray, cold Christmas Day.

IV.

Then the master said: "Your axes wield,
  Remember ye Malabarre Bay;
And the covenant there with the Lord ye sealed;
  Let your axes ring to-day.
You may talk of the old towns' bells to-night,
  When your work for the Lord is done,
And your boats return, and the shallop's light
  Shall follow the light of the sun.
      The sky is cold and gray, —
    And here are no ancient bells to ring,
    No priests to chant, no choirs to sing,
    No chapel of baron, or lord or king,
      This gray, cold Christmas Day.

V.

"If Christ was born on Christmas Day,
  And the day by Him is blest:
Then low at His feet the evergreens lay,
  And cradle His church in the West.
Immanuel waits at the temple gates
  Of the nation to-day ye found,
And the Lord delights in no formal rites;
  To-day let your axes sound!"
      The sky was cold and gray, —
    And there were no ancient bells to ring,
    No priests to chant, no choirs to sing,
    No chapel of baron, or lord or king,
      That gray, cold Christmas Day.

VI.

Their axes rang through the evergreen trees,
  Like the bells on the Thames and Tay:
And they cheerily sung by the windy seas,
  And they thought of Malabarre Bay.

On the lonely heights of Burial Hill
  The old Precisioners sleep;
But did ever men with a nobler will,
  A holier Christmas keep
    When the sky was cold and gray, —
    And there were no ancient bells to ring,
    No priests to chant, no choirs to sing,
    No chapel of baron, or lord or king,
    That gray, cold Christmas Day?

THE ROSES OF RHODES.

[RHODE ISLAND.]

In the tides of the warm south wind it lay,
  And its grapes turned wine in the fires of noon,
And its roses blossomed from May to May,
  And their fragrance lingered from June to June.

There dwelt old heroes at Ilium famed,
  There, bards reclusive, of olden odes;
And so fair were the fields of roses, they named
  The bright sea garden the Isle of Rhodes.

Fair temples graced each blossoming field,
  And columned halls in gems arrayed;
Night shaded the sea with her jewelled shield,
  And sweet the lyres of Orpheus played.

The Helios spanned the sea: its flame
  Drew hither the ships of Pelion's pines,
And twice a thousand statues of fame
  Stood mute in twice a thousand shrines.

And her mariners went, and her mariners came,
    And sang on the seas the olden odes,
And at night they remembered the Helios' flame,
    And at morn the sweet fields of the roses of Rhodes.

From the palm land's shades to the lands of pines,
    A Florentine crossed the Western sea;
He sought new lands and golden mines,
    And he sailed 'neath the flag of the *Fleur de lis.*

He saw at last, in the sunset's gold,
    A wonderful island so fair to view
That it seemed like the Island of Roses old
    That his eyes in his wondering boyhood knew.

'T was summer time, and the glad birds sung
    In the hush of noon in the solitudes;
From the oak's broad arms the green vines hung;
    Sweet odors blew from the resinous woods.

He rounded the shores of the summer sea,
    And he said as his feet the white sands pressed,
And he planted the flag of the *Fleur de lis:*
    " I have come to the Island of Rhodes in the West.

" While the mariners go, and the mariners come,
    And sing on lone waters the olden odes
Of the Grecian seas and the ports of Rome,
    They ever will think of the roses of Rhodes."

To the isle of the West he gave the name
    Of the isle he had loved in the Grecian sea;
And the Florentine went away as he came,
    'Neath the silver flag of the *Fleur de lis.*

O fair Rhode Island, thy guest was true,
  He felt the spirit of beauteous things;
Thy sea-wet roses were faint and few,
  But memory made them the gardens of kings.

The Florentine corsair sailed once more,
  Out into the West o'er a rainy sea,
In search of another wonderful shore
  For the crown of France and the *Fleur de lis.*

But returned no more the Florentine brave
  To the courtly knights of fair Rochelle;
'Neath the lilies of France he found a grave,
  And not 'neath the roses he loved so well.

But the lessons of beauty his fond heart bore
  From the gardens of God were never lost;
And the fairest name of the Eastern shore
  Bears the fairest isle of the Western coast.

7

THE BIRD WITH A BROKEN WING.

I WALKED in the woodland meadows,
  Where sweet the thrushes sing;
And I found on a bed of mosses
  A bird with a broken wing.

I healed the wound; and each morning
  It sang its old sweet strain.
But the bird with a broken pinion
  Never soared as high again.

I found a youth, life-broken
  By sin's seductive art ;
And, touched with Christ-like pity,
  I took him to my heart.
He lived with a noble purpose,
  And struggled not in vain.
But the soul with a broken pinion
  Never soars as high again.

But the bird with a broken pinion
  Kept another from the snare ;
And the life that sin had stricken
  Raised another from despair.
Each loss had its compensation :
  There were healings for each pain ;
But a bird with a broken pinion
  Never soars as high again.

THE BEAUTIFUL VILLAGE OF YULE.

My spring-time of life has de-
    parted ;
Its romance has ended at last:
My dreamings were once of the
    future,
    But now they are all of the
    past.
And memory oft in my trials
    Goes back to my pastimes at
    school,
And pictures the children who
    loved me
    In the beautiful village of Yule.

The schoolhouse still stands by
    the meadow,
    And green is the spot where
    I played,
And flecked with the sun is the
    shadow
    Of the evergreen woods where
    I strayed.
The thrush in the meadowy
    places
    Still sings in the evergreens
    cool ;
But changed are the fun-loving
    faces
    Of the children who met me
    at Yule.

I remember the day, when, a teacher,
  I met those dear faces anew;
The warm-hearted greetings that told me
  The friendships of childhood are true.
I remember the winters I struggled,
  When careworn and sick, in my school:
I remember the children who loved me
  In the beautiful village of Yule.

So true, in the days of my sadness,
  Did the hearts of my trusted ones prove,
My sorrow grew light in the gladness
  Of having so many to love.
I gave my own heart to my scholars,
  And banished severity's rule;
And happiness dwelt in my schoolroom,
  In the beautiful village of Yule.

I taught them the goodness of loving
  The beauty of nature and art;
They taught me the goodness of loving
  The beauty that lies in the heart.
And I prize more than lessons of knowledge
  The lessons I learned in my school,—
The warm hearts that met me at morning,
  And left me at evening, in Yule.

I remember the hour that we parted:
  I told them, while moistened my eye,
That the bell of the schoolroom of glory
  Would ring for us each in the sky.
Their faces were turned to the sunset,
  As they stood 'neath the evergreens cool:
I shall see them no more as I saw them,
  In the beautiful village of Yule.

The bells of the schoolroom of glory
    Their summons have rung in the sky.
The moss and the fern of the valley
    On some of the old pupils lie :
Some have gone from the wearisome studies
    Of earth to the happier school ;
Some faces are bright with the angels',
    Who stood in the sunset at Yule.

I love the instructions of knowledge,
    The teachings of nature and art,
But more than all others the lessons
    That come from an innocent heart.
And still to be patient and loving
    And trustful I hold as a rule.
For so I was taught by the children
    Of the beautiful village of Yule.

My spring-time of life has departed ;
    Its romance has ended at last :
My dreamings were once of the future,
    But now they are all of the past.
Methinks when I stand in life's sunset,
    As I stood when we parted at school,
I shall see the bright faces of scholars
    I loved in the village of Yule.

LINCOLN'S LAST DREAM.

I.

April flowers were in the hollows ; in the air were April bells.
And the wings of purple swallows rested on the battle shells.
From the war's long scene of horror now the nation found
   release ;
All the day the old war bugles blew the blessed notes of peace.
      'Thwart the twilight's damask curtains
      Fell the night upon the land,
      Like God's smile of benediction
      Shadowed faintly by his hand.
In the twilight. in the dusklight, in the starlight, everywhere,
Banners waved like gardened flowers in the palpitating air.

II.

In Art's temple there were greetings, gentle hurryings of feet.
And triumphant strains of music rose amid the numbers sweet.
Soldiers gathered. heroes gathered, women beautiful were there :
Will *he* come, the land's Beloved, there to rest an hour from
   care ?
      Will he come who for the people
      Long the cross of pain has borne. —
      Prayed in silence, wept in silence,
      Held the hand of God alone ?
Will he share the hour of triumph, now his mighty work is
   done ?
Here receive the people's plaudits, now the victory is won ?

III.

O'er thy dimpled waves, Potomac, softly now the moonbeams
    creep;
O'er far Arlington's green meadows, where the brave forever sleep.
'Tis Good Friday; bells are tolling, bells of chapels beat the air
On thy quiet shores, Potomac; Arlington, serene and fair.
    And he comes, the nation's hero,
      From the White House, worn with care;
    Hears the name of " Lincoln !" ringing
      In the thronged streets, everywhere :
Hears the bells, — what memories bringing to his long-uplifted
    heart!
Hears the plaudits of the people as he gains the Hall of Art.

IV.

Throbs the air with thrilling music, gayly onward sweeps the
    play :
But he little heeds the laughter, for his thoughts are far away ;
And he whispers faintly, sadly, " Oft a blessed Form I see,
Walking calmly 'mid the people on the shores of Galilee;
    Oft I've wished His steps to follow.
      Gently listen, wife of mine !
    When the cares of State are over,
      I will go to Palestine,
And the paths the Blessed followed I will walk from sea to sea,
Follow Him who healed the people on the shores of Galilee."

V.

Hung the flag triumphant o'er him; and his eyes with tears were
    dim,
Though a thousand eyes before him lifted oft their smiles to him.
Forms of statesmen, forms of heroes, women beautiful were there.
But it was another vision that had calmed his brow of care :

Tabor glowed in light before him,
    Carmel in the evening sun;
Faith's strong armies grandly marching
    Through the vale of Esdralon;
Bethany's palm-shaded gardens, where the Lord the sisters met,
And the Pascal moon arising o'er the brow of Olivet.

VI.

Now the breath of light applauses rose the templed arches through,
Stirred the folds of silken banners, mingled red and white and
    blue;
But the Dreamer seemed to heed not: rose the past his eye
    before, —
Armies guarding the Potomac, flashing through the Shenandoah;
    Gathering armies, darkening navies,
        Heroes marching forth to die;
    Chickamauga, Chattanooga,
        And the Battle of the Sky;
Silent prayers to free the bondmen in the ordeal of fire,
And God's angel's sword uplifted to fulfil his heart's desire.

VII.

Thought he of the streets of Richmond on the late triumphant
    day
When the swords of vanquished leaders at his feet surrendered
    lay;
When, amid the sweet bells ringing, all the sable multitudes
Shouted forth the name of " Lincoln! " like a rushing of the
    floods;
        Thought of all his heart had suffered;
        All his struggles and renown;
        Dreaming not that just above him
        Lifted was the martyr's crown;
Seeing not the dark form stealing through the music-haunted air;
Knowing not that 'mid the triumph the betrayer's feet were there.

VIII.

April morning; flags are blowing; 'thwart each flag a sable bar.
Dead, the leader of the people; dead, the world's great commoner.
Bells on the Potomac tolling; tolling by the Sangamon;
Tolling from the broad Atlantic to the Ocean of the Sun.
  Friend and foe clasp hands in silence,
   Listen to the low prayers said,
  Hear the people's benedictions,
   Hear the nations praise the dead.
Lovely land of Palestina! he thy shores will never see,
But, his dream fulfilled, he follows Him who walked in Galilee.

TIME MAKES CHANGES PLEASANTLY.

Does trouble rise, and life appear
  A prison with no open gate,
And fettered circumstance and fear
  Attend thy ways?—In silence wait
And look to God: it well will be,
For time makes changes pleasantly.

Let no corroding passions rise
  To vent hot words to add to pain:
Warm lies the light in Southern skies
  To chase the clouds of winter rain;
And heart-content awaits for thee,
For time makes changes pleasantly.

For time the man of peace befriends,
  Removes in silence what appears
Life's boundary wall, and far extends
  The boundaries of future years.
Misfortune tides an influent sea,
And time makes changes pleasantly.

THE OLD FLOWER BEDS 'NEATH THE WINDOWS.

[EASTER.]

I.

To the old home farm returning
  'Mid the sunset's lights and glooms,
I kiss the faces that knew me,
  And I turn to the vacant rooms.
The scenes of my long-gone childhood
  The doors that I open recall,
The blossoming windows of summer,
  The fruit-laden orchards of fall.

The light purple wings of the swallows
  Are gemmed in the sunset as then,
And still seeks the fairy-like hollows
  Of the yellow gourd-houses, the wren.

III.

I go to a tenantless chamber;
  The moon glimmers over the eaves,
And a light, as in years long vanished,
  In the latticed window leaves.
And, in fancy, night's viewless angel
  Goes by with a muffled tread,
As I gaze with an answerless longing
  On the little one's empty bed.

IV.

There were little blue eyes that forever
  Have vanished from my sight;
A heart of affection that never
  Will throb on my own with delight.
I shall never again kneel beside him,
  I shall pray in the silence instead.
Fall gently, O dews, in the graveyard.
  Where the green myrtles cover his bed.

V.

My hand-in-hand companion,
  That the years will never restore,
The little lost hand 'neath the mosses
  Will lock in my fingers no more!
As the moonlight all white is the pillow
  Where rested a curl-circled head;
And the April winds sigh through the willow
  That waves o'er the little one's bed.

VI.

O dear little lips that no longer
  In love will be lifted to mine!
O dear little arms that grew stronger,
  My neck in their ring to entwine!
Each place, gentle heart, where I loved thee,
  Is sprinkled with tears I have shed.
And the glow of lost years of affection
  Comes back as I gaze on thy bed.

VII.

I think of the gardens immortal,
  And I seem in a vision to see
A little hand open the portal
  That life has long hidden from me.
Still they bloom, the old flowers 'neath the window,
  And I say, "Can my darling be dead?"
Or do I behold but the pillow
  Where a bright angel rested, and fled?

WHEN MY CHILDREN WERE ABOUT ME.

O that I were as in months past, as in the days when God preserved me ;
When His candle shined upon my head, and when by His light I walked through darkness ;
As I was in the days of my youth, when the secret of God was upon my tabernacle.
When the Almighty was yet with me, when my children were about me. — JOB xxix. 2–5.

I.

GREEN springs return, the swallows come,
　And croon the golden bees ;
Suave summers bring their fluting winds
　To blossom-clouded trees.
Life's spring and summer have their prime ;
　And, looking back, with tears
I ask, What is the happiest time
　Of life's eventful years ?

II.

The happiest time ? — I turn the page,
　I read the Hebrew seer,
Who saw, in grief, the Golden Age
　That Memory holds most dear ;
Not when high Youth expectant peers
　To Hope's cerulean skies,
Nor in the calm of withered years
　When disenchantment sighs.

III.

'T was in that blossom-haunted time
  'Neath life's meridian beam.
When homely virtues have their prime
  And fill the heart's fond dream.
Then rose the golden days, again
  As bright to reappear:
" My children were about me then,
  And GOD Himself was near."

IV.

Where sweet Affection makes her tent
  There shine the stars serene:
The lilied airs have sweeter scent,
  The earth a deeper green.
By frigid sea or sunlit palms
  No memory is so dear
As children clasped in loving arms,
  And God's own presence near.

V.

The merchant gleans the earth, and stores
  The fruits the nations reap,
From spicy port and icy shores,
  And isle-bejewelled deep.
His bright bazaars uplift their wings
  By either sail-swept sea:
'T is more than *wealth* to be beloved
  By children at the knee.

VI.

The poet seeks fame's storied land
  To feel romance's sway:
And, tranced beneath Night's jewelled hand,
  He hears the low lutes play.

"'Twas in that blossom-haunted time
'Neath life's meridian beam."

He curves the burning Indian shore,
  The dark Ægean Sea :
'T is more than *fame* to be beloved
  By children at the knee.

VII.

The traveller treads the cities old
  'Mid monuments of art,
But finds, 'neath cupolas of gold,
  No market of the heart.
Love is not bought, love is not sold,
  By any purpling sea :
'T is *home-content* to be beloved
  By children at the knee.

VIII.

And so I answer, as I dream
  Of life's most happy time :
Full oft it comes, like sweet June days,
  In virtuous manhood's prime.
As this, in after days shall be
  No memory so dear,
With loving children at the knee,
  And God's own presence near.

THE PATRIOT'S REMEMBRANCES.

SWEET spring is in the air, good wife,
   The bluer sky appears,
The robin sings the welcome note
   He sung in other years.
Twelve times the spring has oped the rills,
   Twelve times has autumn sighed,
Since hung the war clouds o'er the hills,
   The year that Lincoln died.

The March wind early left the zone
   For distant northern seas,
And wandering airs of gentle tone
   Came to the door-yard trees;
And sadness in the dewy hours
   Her reign extended wide
When spring retouched the hills with flowers,
   The year that Lincoln died.

We used to sit and talk of him,
    Our long, long absent son;
We'd two to love us then, good wife,
    But now we have but one.
The springs return, the autumns burn
    His grave unknown beside;
They laid him 'neath the moss and fern,
    The year that Lincoln died.

One day I was among the flocks
    That roamed the April dells,
When floating from the city came
    The sound of many bells.
The towns around caught up the sound;
    I climbed the mountain side,
And saw the spires with banners crowned,
    The year that Lincoln died.

I knew what meant that sweet accord,
    That jubilee of bells,
And sang an anthem to the Lord
    Amid the pleasant dells.
But when I thought of those so young
    That slept the James beside,
In undertones of joy I sung,
    The year that Lincoln died.

And when the tidings came, good wife,
    Our soldier boy was dead,
I bowed my trembling knee in prayer,
    You bowed your whitened head.
The house was still, the woods were calm,
    Fair was the eventide:
I sang alone the evening psalm,
    The year that Lincoln died.

I hung his picture 'neath the shelf:
   It still is hanging there;
I laid his ring where you yourself
   Had put a curl of hair.
Then to the spot where willows wave
   With hapless steps we hied,
And " Charley's " called an empty grave,
   The year that Lincoln died.

The years will come, the years will go,
   But never at our door
The fair-haired boy we used to meet
   Will smile upon us more.
But memory long will hear the fall
   Of steps at eventide,
And every blooming year recall
   The year that Lincoln died.

One day I was among the flocks
   That roamed the April dells,
When at the noonday hour I heard
   A tolling of the bells.
With heavy heart and footsteps slow
   I climbed the mountain side,
And saw the blue flags hanging low,
   The year that Lincoln died.

That eve I stopped to rest awhile
   Beside the meadow bars,
Where, years before, poor Charley watched
   The comet 'mong the stars.
Then from his night-encumbered way
   A traveller stepped aside;
And told the news that fateful day,
   The year that Lincoln died.

" The bells that rung when Richmond fell
    Are tolling all," he said;
" Hark ! hear ye not your village bell ?
    It tolls for Lincoln dead.
He who his birthright gave the slave
    And right to right allied.
Has won the martyr's name and grave."
    I wept when Lincoln died.

Peace smiles upon the hills and dells,
    Peace smiles upon the seas ;
And drop the notes of happy bells
    Upon the fruited trees.
The broad Missouri stretches far
    Her commerce-gathering arms,
And multiply on Arkansas
    The grain-encumbered farms.

In dreams I stand beside the tide ;
    Where those old heroes fell,
Above the valleys, long and wide,
    Sweet rings the Sabbath bell.
I hear no more the bugle blow.
    As on that fateful day :
I hear the ring-dove fluting low,
    Where shaded waters stray.

On Mission Ridge the sunlight streams
    Above the fields of fall,
And Chattanooga calmly dreams
    Beneath her mountain wall.
Old Lookout Mountain towers on high,
    As in heroic days,
When 'neath the battle in the sky
    Was seen its summit's blaze.

But many a year, ah! many a year,
  The birds will cross the seas,
And blossoms fall in gentle showers
  Beneath the door-yard trees;
And still will tender mothers weep
  The soldiers' graves beside,
And fresh in memory ever keep
  The year that Lincoln died.

Where many sow the seed in tears
  Shall many reap in joy;
And harvesters in golden years
  Shall ever bless our boy.
With happy homes for other eyes
  Expands the future wide;
And God will bless our sacrifice,
  The year that Lincoln died.

MEETING AND PARTING.

Written on the Terrace, Quebec.

[NEW YEAR'S.]

ALONE, beside these peaceful guns
   I walk, — the eve is calm and fair.
Below, the broad St. Lawrence runs;
   Above, the castle shines in air;
And o'er the breathless sea and land
Night stretches forth her jewelled hand.

Amid the crowds that hurry past —
   Bright faces like a sunlit tide —
Some eyes the gifts of friendship cast
   Upon me, as I walk aside, —
Kind, wordless welcomes understood,
The Spirit's touch of brotherhood.

Below, the sea; above, the sky,
   Smile each to each, a vision fair :
So like Faith's zones of light on high,
   A sphere seraphic seems the air,
And loving thoughts there seem to meet,
And come and go with golden feet.

Below me lies the old French town,
   With narrow streets and churches quaint.
And tilèd roofs and gables brown,
   And signs with names of many a saint.
And there in all I see appears
The heart of twice an hundred years.

Beyond, by inky steamers mailed.
  Point Levi's painted roofs arise,
Where emigration long has hailed
  The empires of the western skies:
And lightly wave the red flags there,
Like roses of the damask air.

Peace o'er yon garden spreads her palm,
  Where heroes fought in other days;
And Honor speaks of brave Montcalm
  On Wolfe's immortal shaft of praise.
What lessons that I used to learn
In schoolboy days to me return!

Fair terrace of the Western Rhine,
  I leave thee with unwilling feet;
1 long shall see thy castle shine
  As bright as now, in memories sweet,
And cheerful thank the kindly eyes
That lent to me their sympathies.

Go, friendly hearts, that met by chance
  A stranger for a little while ;
Friendship itself is but a glance,
  And love is but a passing smile.
I am a pilgrim, — all I meet
Are glancing eyes and hurrying feet.

Farewell ; in dreams I see again
  The northern river of the vine,
While crowns the sun with golden grain
  The hillsides of the greater Rhine.
And here shall grow as years increase
The empires of the Rhine of Peace.

IMMORTALITY.

Written after listening to the Organ Tempest of Lucerne.

[EASTER.]

WE came to fair Lucerne at even, —
  How beauteous was the scene!
The snowy Alps, like walls of heaven,
  Rose o'er the Alps of green;
The damask sky a roseate light
  Flashed on the Lake, and low
Above Mt. Pilate's shadowy height
  Night bent her silver bow.

We turnèd towards the faded fane,
  How many centuries old!
And entered as the organ's strain
  Along the arches rolled;
Such as when guardian spirits bear
  A soul to realms of light,
And melts in the immortal air
  The anthem of their flight;
Then followed strains so sweet,
  So sadly sweet and low,
That they seemed like memory's music,
  And the chords of long ago.

A light wind seemed to rise;
  A deep gust followed soon,
As when a dark cloud flies
  Across the sun, at noon.
It filled the aisles, — each drew
  His garments round his form;
We could not feel the wind that blew,
  But only hear the storm.
Then we cast a curious eye
  Towards the window's lights,
And saw the Lake serenely lie
  Beneath the crystal heights.
Fair rose the Alps of white
  Above the Alps of green;
The slopes lay bright in the sun of night,
  And the peaks in the sun unseen.

A deep sound shook the air,
  As when the tempest breaks
Upon the peaks, while sunshine fair
  Is dreaming in the lakes.
Then like a fateful wing
  There rose a wind so drear,
Its troubled spirit seemed to bring
  The shades of darkness near.
We looked towards the windows old:
  Calm was the eve of June;
On the summits shone the twilight's gold,
  And on Pilate shone the moon.

A sharp note's lightning flash
  Upturned the startled face;
When a mighty thunder-crash
  With horror filled the place!

From arch to arch the peal
    Was echoed loud and long;
Then o'er the pathway seemed to steal
    Another seraph's song;
And 'mid the thunder's crash
    And the song's enraptured flow,
We still could hear, with charmèd ear,
    The organ playing low.

As passed the thunder-peal,
    Came raindrops, falling near,
A rain one could not feel,
    A rain that smote the ear.
And we turned to look again
    Towards the mountain wall,
When a deep tone shook the fane,
    Like the avalanche's fall.
Loud piped the wind, fast poured the rain,
    The very earth seemed riven,
And wildly flashed, and yet again,
    The smiting fires of heaven.

And cheeks that wore the light of smiles
    When slowly rose the gale,
Like pulseless statues lined the aisles
    And, as forms of marble, pale.
The organ's undertones
    Still sounded sweet and low,
And the calm of a more than mortal trust
    With the rhythms seemed to flow.

The Master's mirrored face
    Was lifted from the keys,
As if more holy was the place
    As he touched the notes of peace.

Then the sympathetic reeds
  The sweet enchantment wrought,
As the senses met the needs
  And the touch of human thought.
The organ whispered sweet,
  The organ whispered low,
" Fear not, God's love is with thee.
  Though tempests round thee blow!"
And the soul's grand power 't was ours to trace,
  And its deathless hopes discern,
As we gazed that night on the living face
  Of the Organ of Lucerne.

Then from the church it passed,
  That strange and ghostly storm,
And a parting beam the twilight cast
  Through the windows, bright and warm.

The music grew more clear,
  Our gladdened pulses swaying,
When Alpine horns we seemed to hear
  On all the hillsides playing.

We left the church: how fair
  Stole on the eve of June!
Cool Righi in the dusky air.
  The low-descending moon!
No breath the lake cerulean stirred;
  No cloud could eye discern;
The Alps were silent: we had heard
  The Organ of Lucerne.

Soon passed the night: the high peaks shone
  A wall of glass and fire,
And Morning, from her summer zone,
  Illumined tower and spire;
I walked beside the lake again,
  Along the Alpine meadows;
Then sought the old melodious fane
  Beneath the Righi's shadows.
The organ, spanned by arches quaint.
  Rose silent, cold, and bare,
Like the pulseless tomb of a vanished saint: —
  The Master was not there!
But the soul's grand power 't was mine to trace
  And its deathless hopes discern.
As I gazed that morn on the still, dead face
  Of the Organ of Lucerne.

"YE DID IT UNTO ME."

I KNOW not when the lamps of God
  Should light the Christmas shrine;
The Volga's bells do not accord
  With those upon the Rhine;
But when the bells of either clime
  Ring out for charity,
Their tongues melodious seem to chime:
  "Ye did it unto Me!"

That psalm that, 'mid December's snows,
  We sing with joy to-day,
In Eastern chapels erst arose,
  In the bright month of May.
It matters not. The deeds of old
  With those to-day agree:
The poor man shares the rich man's gold:
  "Ye did it unto Me!"

The time, the date, is little worth
  If heart to heart accord,
And but the suffering ones of earth
  Receive the gold of God.
The semblance of the Lord is met
  In every Christmas-tree,
And heard the words of Olivet:
  "Ye did it unto Me!"

In every ministry to woe,
  In every help to pain,
The sandalled feet of Jesus go,
  As once they went to Nain;
Bread multiplied we may behold
  In every charity,
As at Decapolis of old:
  "Ye did it unto Me!"

Chime on, ye bells! In every clime
  The angels' strain uplift;
It is the spirit, not the time,
  That sanctifies the gift!
The Christ-child with the children comes
  To every Christmas-tree
Or by the Rhine's or Neva's homes:
  "Ye did it unto Me!"

Then light again the Yule log's fires,
  And bring your Christmas dowers,
Although the white Muscovian spires
  May not accord with ours;
And He will walk again with men,
  Who walked in Galilee;
And His sweet voice will say again:
  "Ye did it unto Me!"

THE FISHERMAN OF FAROE.

WHEN life was young, my white sail hung
O'er ocean's crystal floor;
In the fiords alee was the dreaming sea,
And the deep sea waves before.
The Faroe fishermen used to call
From the pier's extremest post:
"Strike out, my boy, from the ocean wall;
There's danger near the coast.
Beware of the drifting dunes
In the nights of the watery moons,
Beware of the Maelstrom's tide
When the western wind blows free,
Of the rocks of the Skagerrack,
Of the shoals of the Cattegat;
Strike out for the open sea,
Strike out for the open sea!"

"O pilot! pilot! every rock
You know in the ocean wall."
"No, no, my boy, I only know
Where there are no rocks at all,

Where there are no rocks at all, my boy,
　And there no ship is lost.
Strike out, strike out for the open sea;
　There's danger near the coast.
　　Beware, I say, of the dunes
　　In the nights of the watery moons,
　　　Beware of the Maelstrom's tide
　When the western wind blows free,
　Of the rocks of the Skagerrack,
　Of the shoals of the Cattegat;
　Strike out for the open sea,
　Strike out for the open sea!"

Low sunk the trees in the sun-laved seas,
　And the flash of peaking oars
Grew faint and dim on the sheeny rim
　Of the harbor-dented shores.
And far Faroe in the light lay low,
　Where rode like a dauntless host
The white-plumed waves o'er the green sea graves
　Of the rock-imperilled coast.
　　And I thought of the drifting dunes
　　In the nights of the watery moons,
　　　And I thought of the Maelstrom's tide
　When the western wind blew free,
　Of the rocks of the Skagerrack,
　Of the shoals of the Cattegat,
　And I steered for the open sea,
　I steered for the open sea.

To far Faroe I sailed away,
　When bright the summer burned,
And I told in the old Norse kirk one day
　The lesson my heart had learned.

"And the ship goes down in sight of the town
That sate the deep sea tides."

Then the grizzly landvogt said to me:
"Of strength we may not boast;
But ever in life for you and me
  There's danger near the coast.
    Then think of the drifting dunes
    In the nights of the watery moons,
      And think of the Maelstrom's tide
    When the western wind blows free,
    Of the rocks of the Skagerrack,
    Of the shoals of the Cattegat;
    Strike out for the open sea,
    Strike out for the open sea!"

"O landvogt, well thou knowest the ways
  Wherein my feet may fall."
"Oh, no, my boy, I only know
  The ways that are safe to all,
The ways that are safe to all, my boy,
  And there no soul is lost.
Strike out in life for the open sea,
  There's danger near the coast.
    Then think of the drifting dunes
    In the nights of the watery moons,
      And think of the Maelstrom's tide
    When the western wind blows free,
    Of the rocks of the Skagerrack,
    Of the shoals of the Cattegat:
    Strike out for the open sea,
    Strike out for the open sea!

"False lights, false lights, are near the land.
  The reef the land wave hides,
And the ship goes down in sight of the town
  That safe the deep sea rides.

'T is those who steer the old life near
Temptation suffer most;
The way is plain to life's open main,
There 's danger near the coast.
     Beware of the drifting dunes
     In the nights of the watery moons,
          Beware of the Maelstrom's tide
     When the western wind blows free,
     Of the rocks of the Skagerrack,
     Of the shoals of the Cattegat;
     Strike out for the open sea,
     Strike out for the open sea!"

And so on life's sea I sailed away,
     Where free the waters flow,
As I sailed from the old home port that day
     For the islands of far Faroe.
And when I steer temptation near,
     The pilot, like a ghost,
On the wave-rocked pier I seem to hear:
     "There 's danger near the coast.
     Beware of the drifting dunes
     In the nights of the watery moons,
          Beware of the Maelstrom's tide
     When the western wind blows free,
     Of the rocks of the Skagerrack,
     Of the shoals of the Cattegat;
     Strike out for the open sea,
     Strike out for the open sea!"

OLD CLASS-ROOM NUMBER FOUR.

AN OLD FRIEND'S STORY DURING A WALK.

THE light is warm on Newton's hills
    With halls of learning crowned:
The sunset shadow, lengthening, fills
    The memory-haunted ground.
O bowery heights! O sun-lit peaks!
    My eye to you once more
Is turned, and, dim with feeling, seeks
What once it sought with glowing cheeks,
    Old class-room Number Four.

'T is autumn, and an amber haze,
    An over-sea of gold,
Is bright as in the olden days,
    And has the charm of old.
The birds are gone, the cricket sings
    Upon the grassy floor,
And quickened thought its vision brings
Of vanished youth and withered springs,
    And class-room Number Four.

I walk the upward path alone
    That once I walked with friends;
A pilgrim to the halls alone
    My halting step ascends.

I see the pine-plumed hill-tops rise
    Around me as of yore;
Below, the weir, cloud-shadowed, lies;
Above, the blue lakes of the skies;
    The silent halls, before.

O shaded windows that I see
    By pilgrim years endeared,
Where oft I dreamed, and fair to me
    The future's light appeared;

Lawns, where I used to sport and play
  With classmates seen no more,
Springless and summerless to-day
I wend alone life's autumn way
  To class-room Number Four.

Where are they now, where are they now,—
  The friends who gathered there,
And oft, with faith-illumined brow,
  Spoke of the future fair?
Where are the ardent hands that met
  Each evening at the door?
My life is green in memory yet,
But never can my heart forget
  Old class-room Number Four.

One sleeps beside the mobile seas,—
  His life had just begun.—
And one beneath yon crimsoned trees
  Who died for Aracan.
Kind Nature spreads the grass and fern
  The graves of others o'er;
The flamed-tipped leaves above them burn;
Their feet, alas! will ne'er return
  To class-room Number Four.

We toil and sow, but only gain
  The harvests of our prayers;
Our hopes in God alone remain
  Of all our anxious cares.
To these, how little worth appears
  The all of learning's store,
The classic lore, the thoughts of seers,
I gathered in those early years
  I spent in Number Four.

The light is low. the sunset's glow
  Scarce hides the evening star,
And winds through dreamy shades below,
  The silver Charles afar.
Farewell! O shadow-mantled halls!
  I ne'er may see you more;
Afar the voice of duty calls,
As sombre night around me falls
  And class-room Number Four.

NEW YEAR'S HYMN.

(Written for Ruggles Street Church Anniversary, 1875.)

FOR us, O Lord, the year has brought
    Its bloom and harvest glory;
To us, through changing seasons, taught
    Thy truth, in Gospel story.
Again our voices join in song,
    And bring their glad thanksgiving
To Thee, to whom all years belong,
    To Thee, the ever-living.

We meet with gladness on each lip,
    And kindly warmth of greeting,
And in Thy boundless fellowship,
    Each heart to heart is beating.
And for this day, and for this hour,
    We bring our glad thanksgiving
To Thee, the ever gracious Lord,
    To Thee, the ever-living.

We oft have sung with fresh delight
    Of thy new love upspringing,
And some who joined our songs, to-night
    Are with the angels singing.

But friends below and friends above
  Unite in glad thanksgiving
To Thee, whom all thy children love,
  To Thee, the ever-living.

Thy power in prayer we oft have felt,
  Thy sympathy most tender,
And seemed to see, as we have knelt,
  Thy face in veilèd splendor.
For all these joys from Paradise,
  We bring our glad thanksgiving
To Thee, who every good supplies,
  To Thee, the ever-living.

So may we join from year to year,
  Thy goodness ever singing,
And after faithful service, hear
  The bells of glory ringing.
Then, safe with Thee, again we'll raise
  Our voices in thanksgiving
To Thee, in more exalted praise,
  To Thee, the ever-living.

THE FLAG OF FORTY STARS.

I WALKED in Arlington's lone fields near even :
 The wings of Night drew nigh ;
While half the sun, like a far gate of heaven,
 Burned in the autumn sky.

No more the lawns with fountain spray were christened ;
 But, 'neath the glimmering domes,
Far in the purpling light the city glistened,
 A wilderness of homes.

On crisping leaves was Nature's pen inditing
 The lesson of the fall,
Seeming almost like that mysterious writing
 In Babel's banquet-hall.

Around me rose white monuments in clusters,
 An open space before,
Where graves reflect few monumental lustres, —
 A sad field of Manoah.

It is the field of single graves, where slumber
 Young heroes 'neath the mounds ;
And yet " Unknown " on tablets without number
 I read in those broad grounds.

There heroes sleep. Balm-breathing Junes returning
  Touch with wild flowers their bed;
And fair years pass, with golden harvest burning,
  Above the unknown dead.

To think of them the gay world seldom pauses;
  They had in it no part:
In life they gained no feverish applauses,
  In death, no shaft of art.

I said to one I met, a soldier lonely,
  With sorrow in my eyes,
"Brave men lie here;" and then I added, "Only
  How great the sacrifice!"

Toward the Potomac and the Capitol turning,
　　Then said the man of scars,
"I see, amid the twilight hazes burning,
　　The Flag of Forty Stars.

"The blue Potomac hears no battle-marches;
　　The fruiting fields increase;
And Plenty piles her stores to heaven's arches,
　　And all the land is Peace."

Night's curtain fell, the distant city shading:
　　I left the field of Mars;
But long I saw above the Capitol fading
　　The Flag of Forty Stars.

A NEW YEAR'S PRAYER.

By all that I to others owe,
  By all I hope to prove,
By all that other lives bestow
  On mine, of hope and love,
By all my influence, day by day,
  Whose end I cannot see,
Lord, take, forever take away,
  My wrong desires from me!

By what I owe a mother's love,
  By what a father's care,
By all to honor I would prove,
  And all for virtue bear,
From lapse from good, from passion's sway,
  Oh, keep my spirit free,
And take, forever take away,
  My wrong desires from me!

By all the magnitude of loss
  To those who fail and fall,
By all I owe my Saviour's cross
  To which for help I call;
By all I owe to souls astray
  That would direction see,
Oh, take, forever take away,
  My wrong desires from me!

"TO THE RIGHT, TO THE RIGHT EVER TRUE."

Ode written for the One Hundred and Forty-ninth Anniversary of the Ancient and Honorable Artillery.

[PATRIOTIC.]

I.

WAKE the song to the nation's defenders,
  The years of prosperity glow;
The natal day welcome that renders
  The love that to valor we owe;
Wake the song where our fathers, undaunted,
  Proclaimed, when the nation was new,
That their ensign for Liberty planted
  Should be to the Right ever true!

Chorus.

To the Right, to the Right ever true,
To the Right, to the Right ever true,
  The ensign for Liberty planted
Should be to the Right ever true.

II.

When the Red Cross of England contended
  With the Lilies of France, in their might
Our fathers arose and defended
  For freedom the cause of the Right;

Then dared they the sceptre to sever;
  For the Right, the far forest ways trod,
And templed the fair hills, wherever
  Their faces were lifted to God.

Chorus.

To the Right, to the Right ever true,
To the Right, to the Right ever true,
  The ensign for Liberty planted
Has been to the Right ever true.

III.

The banners of tyranny faded,
  The Red Cross and Lilies of Gold,
And the folds no oppression had shaded —
  The stars of the empire — unrolled!
And they pledged it, these heroes victorious,
  As on Liberty's breeze it unfurled,
To the birthright of man, ever glorious,
  And to freemen, the Kings of the world!

Chorus.

To the Right, to the Right ever true,
To the Right, to the Right ever true,
  The ensign for Liberty planted
Has been to the Right ever true.

IV.

Her red war when Slavery vaunted,
  The heroes of Right rose as one,
The banner the father had planted
  Was guarded for Right by the son.
Young martyrs, — let valor deplore them. —
  Their names on the white marbles glow,
The roses of June redden o'er them,
  The war bugles peacefully blow.

Chorus.

To the Right, to the Right ever true,
To the Right, to the Right ever true,
   The Flag they defended, forever
To the cause of the Right shall be true.

V.

Again at this altar that binds us,
   The faith of the past we 'll renew,—
An hundred years fading behind us,
   A thousand years rising to view.
And as long as the fair constellations
   Shall lighten the heavens with gold,
Shall the banner of Right be the nation's,
   And ever for Right be unrolled!

Chorus.

To the Right, to the Right ever true,
To the Right, to the Right ever true,
   The flag of our nation forever
To the cause of the Right shall be true.

ON THE ATLANTIC.

My God! on seas of storm and calm,
  I pass the ocean o'er,
And sing to thee my thankful psalm,
  Each evening nearer shore.

  Thine is the storm, thine is the calm,
    Wherever I may be;
  And nothing shall my soul alarm
    Upon the silent sea.

A voyager o'er a restless sea,
  I pass to ports divine;
I know bright shores, all waiting me.
  Beyond the horizon line.

I know, for, in the calm of prayer,
  I've seen the fair skies glow,
And felt, through life's reluctant air,
  Immortal breezes blow.

And often, as my spirit sings,
  As calms succeed the gales,
Fair birds, with sunshine on their wings,
  Drift past the restful sails.

When day declines, and thoughts of death
　Come o'er me like a dream,
I dip my golden cup of faith
　In life's celestial stream.

I have an everlasting home,
　Or be it near or far;
My Lord is mine, whate'er may come, —
　He is my Polar Star.

STEAMSHIP "CIRCASSIAN."

" UNKNOWN."

Or where the ring-dove's notes, sweet summer's augur,
    Float from the hillsides o'er the Tennessee,
Or by the James, or by the Chickamauga,
    Or where the Gulf winds dip the sails alee,

Or where the Schuylkill cleaves the vernal shadows,
    Or stretches far the commerce-gathering arms
Of the broad Hudson, through the freshened meadows
    Of village rims and harvest-blooming farms,

Where'er we meet the friends once fondly cherished,
    And hands all warm with old affection take,
Breathe ye with love the names of those who perished
    And sleep in graves unknown, for Freedom's sake.

The wooded slope of Chattanooga shadows
    The level fields where they repose, alone;
In serried rows in Arlington's green meadows,
    Their headstones speak the one sad word, "*Unknown.*"

Balm-breathing Junes, to old home-farms returning,
    Bear from green fields no pleasant airs to them,
Nor rose and lily's odorous censers burning
    In morning suns, from dew-bejewelled stem.

The west winds blow by Chickamauga River,
 The south winds play the Rapidan beside ;
But they are dead, and we shall see them never,
 Till heaven's armies follow Him who died.

Peace! Let us mingle love's sweet tears with pity's
 For those who bought the heritage we own,
Who gave their all, and in death's silent cities
 Have but the nameless epitaph, *Unknown.*